D0502626

The House With Six Legs

and

Other Stories

by
ENID BLYTON

Illustrated by
Ivan Gerald

AWARD PUBLICATIONS LIMITED

For further information on Enid Blyton please contact
www.blyton.com

ISBN 1-84135-010-9

This compilation text copyright © 2000 The Enid Blyton Company
Illustrations copyright © 2000 Award Publications Limited

Enid Blyton's signature is a trademark of
The Enid Blyton Company

This edition entitled *The House With Six Legs and Other Stories*
published by permission of The Enid Blyton Company

This edition first published 2000

Published by Award Publications Limited,
27 Longford Street, London NW1 3DZ

Printed in Singapore

and I'm not strong enough to get it out all by myself."

Jill and Nicky were only too ready to help. Nicky held up one side of the house while the house lifted up one of its feet to have its big shoe taken off. The pixie and Jill found a big stone in the shoe, and after they had shaken it out they put on the shoe again. The little house made a

had caught up to the limping house. Just as they got near it the door opened and a pixie looked out. She was very lovely, for her long golden hair was as fine as spiders' thread, and her wings shone like dragonfly wings.

"What's the matter, little house?" they heard her say. "Why are you limping?"

Then she saw the children and she stared at them in surprise.

"Oh, so that's why the houses ran off!" she said. "They saw you coming! Could you help me, please, children? I think my house has a stone in one of its shoes,

CONTENTS

The House
With Six Legs

If it hadn't been for Puppydog Pincher
the adventure would never have
happened. Jill and Nicky were taking him
for a walk in Cuckoo Wood, and he was
mad with joy. He tore here, there and
everywhere, barking and jumping for all
he was worth.

The children laughed at him, especially
when he tumbled head over heels and
rolled over and over on the grass. He
was such a fat, roly-poly puppy, and they
loved him very much.

Then something happened. Pincher
dived under a bramble bush and came
out with something in his mouth. It was
a string of small sausages!

"Now, wherever could he have got
those from?" said Jill in surprise. She

soon knew, for out from under the bush rushed a little fellow dressed in red and yellow, with a pointed cap on his head. He wasn't much taller than the puppy, but he had a very big voice.

"You bad dog!" he shouted. "You've stolen the sausages I bought for dinner! Bring them back at once or I'll turn you into a mouse!"

Pincher took no notice. He galloped about with the sausages, enjoying himself very much. Then he sat down to eat them! That was too much for the small man. He rushed at Pincher and struck him on the nose with a tiny silver stick. At the same time he shouted out a string of peculiar words, so strange that Jill and Nicky felt quite frightened. They knew they were magic words, although they had never heard any before.

And then, before their eyes, Pincher began to grow small! He grew smaller and smaller and smaller and smaller, and at last he was as tiny as a mouse. In fact, he was a mouse, though he didn't know it! He couldn't think what had happened

to him. He scampered up to Jill and Nicky, barking in a funny little mouse-like squeak.

The children were dreadfully upset. They picked up the tiny mouse and stroked him. Then they looked for the little man to ask him if he would please change Pincher back to a dog again.

But he had gone. Not a sign of him or his sausages was to be seen. Nicky crawled under the bramble bush but there was nothing there but dead leaves.

"Oh, Jill, whatever shall we do?" he said. "We can't take Pincher home like this. Nobody would believe he was Pincher, and he might easily be caught by a cat."

Jill began to cry. She did so love Pincher, and it was dreadful to think he was only a mouse now, not a jolly, romping puppydog.

"That must have been a gnome or a brownie," she said wiping her eyes. "Well, Nicky, I'm not going home with Pincher like that. Let's go further into the wood and see if we meet any more little folk. If there's one here there must be others. We'll ask them for help if we meet them."

So they went on down the little winding path. Nicky carried Pincher in his pocket, for there was plenty of room there for the little dog now that he was only a mouse.

After they had gone a good way they saw a strange little house. It had six legs underneath it, and it stood with its back to the children. Nicky caught hold of Jill's arm and pointed to it in amazement. They had never seen a house with legs before.

"Oh!" cried Jill, stopping in surprise. "It's got legs!"

The house gave a jump when it heard Jill's voice, and then, oh goodness me, it ran off! Yes, it really did! You should have seen its little legs twinkling as it scurried away between the trees. The

children were too astonished to run after the house. They stood and stared.

"This is a funny part of Cuckoo Wood," said Nicky. "I say, Jill! Look! There are some more of those houses with legs!"

Jill looked. Sure enough, in a little clearing stood about six more of the strange houses. Each of them had three pairs of legs underneath, and they wore shoes on their big feet. They stood about, sometimes moving a step or two, and even stood on three legs now and again, which made the house they belonged to look very lopsided and odd.

Jill and Nicky walked towards the funny houses – but dear me! – as soon as they were seen those houses took to their heels and ran off as fast as they could! The children ran after them but they couldn't run fast enough.

They were just going to give up when they saw one of the houses stop. It went on again, but it limped badly.

"We could catch up with that one!" said Jill. "Come on, Nicky!"

They ran on and in a few minutes they

creaking noise that sounded just like "Thank you!"

"What a funny house you've got!" said Jill to the pixie.

"What's funny about it?" asked the pixie in surprise, shaking back her long golden hair. "It's just the same as all my friends' houses."

"But it's got legs!" said Nicky. "Where we come from houses don't have legs at all. They just stand square on the ground and never move, once they are built."

"They sound silly sort of houses," said the pixie. "Suppose an enemy came? Why, your house couldn't run away! Mine's a much better house than yours."

"Oh, much better," agreed Jill. "I only wish I lived in a house like this. It would be lovely. You'd go to sleep at night and wake up in a different place in the morning, because the house might wander miles away."

"I say, Pixie, I wonder if you could help us!" Nicky said suddenly. He took the little mouse out of his pocket. "Look! This was our puppydog not long ago and

a nasty little man changed him into a mouse. Could you change him back into a dog again?"

"Oh, no," said the pixie. "You want very strong magic for that. I only know one person who's got the right magic for your mouse and that's High-Hat the giant."

"Where does he live?" Jill asked eagerly.

"Miles away from here," said the pixie. "You have to go to the Rainbow's End, and then fly up to Cloud Castle just half-way up the rainbow."

"Goodness, we couldn't possibly go there," said Jill. "We haven't wings like you, Pixie."

"Well, Dumpy the gnome lives near the Rainbow's End," said the pixie. "He keeps pigs that fly, you know, so he might lend you two of them. But I don't know if High-Hat the giant will help you, even if you go to him. He's a funny-tempered fellow, and if he's in a bad humour he won't do anything for anybody."

"Well, we could try," said Nicky.

"Which is the way to the Rainbow's End?"

"It depends where there's a rainbow today," said the pixie. "I know! I'll get my house to take you there. It always knows the way to anywhere. Come inside and we'll start. You helped me to get the stone out of my house's shoe, and I'd like to help you in return."

The children went inside the house, feeling most excited. Nicky had Pincher the mouse safely in his pocket. Pincher kept barking in his squeaky voice, for he couldn't understand how it was that Jill and Nicky had grown so big! He didn't know that it was himself that had grown small.

The pixie shut the door and told the children to sit down. It was a funny house inside, more like a carriage than a house, for a bench ran all round the wall. A table stood in the middle of the room and on it were some dishes and cups. In a corner a kettle boiled on a stove, and a big grandfather clock ticked in another corner.

The clock had feet underneath it, like the house, and it gave the children quite a fright when it suddenly walked out from its corner, had a look at them and then walked back.

"Don't take any notice of it," said the pixie. "It hasn't any manners, that old clock. Would you like a cup of cocoa and some daffodil biscuits?"

"Ooh, yes, please!" said both the children at once, wondering whatever daffodil biscuits were. The pixie made a big jug of cocoa and put some funny yellow biscuits, the shape of a daffodil trumpet, on a plate. They tasted delicious, and as for the cocoa, it was lovely – not a bit like ordinary cocoa, but

more like chocolate and lemonade mixed together. The children did enjoy their funny meal.

Before the pixie made the cocoa she spoke to her house. "Take us to the Rainbow's End," she said. "And be as quick as you can."

To the children's great delight the house began to run. They felt as if they were on the sea, or on the elephant's back at the zoo, for the house rocked from side to side as it scampered along. Jill looked out of the window. They were soon out of the wood, and came to a town.

"Nicky, look! There are hundreds of fairy folk here!" cried Jill in excitement. So there were – crowds of them, going about shopping, talking and wheeling funny prams with the dearest baby fairies inside. The grandfather clock walked out of its corner to the window too, and trod on Jill's toe. It certainly had no manners, that clock.

They passed right through the town and went up a hill where little blue sheep

were grazing. Looking after them was a little girl who looked exactly like Bo-Peep. The pixie said yes, it really was Bo-Peep. That was where she lived. It was a most exciting journey, and the children were very sorry when they saw a great rainbow in the distance. They knew they were coming to the end of their journey in the walking house.

The little house stopped when it came to one end of the rainbow. The children stepped outside. There was the rainbow, glittering marvellously. It was very, very wide, far wider than a road, and the colours were almost too bright for them to look at.

"Now High-Hat the giant lives half-way up," said the pixie, pointing. "Come along, I'll take you to Dumpy the gnome, and see if he has a couple of pigs to spare for you."

She took them to a squat little house not far from the rainbow. Outside was a big yard and in it were a crowd of very clean pigs, bright pink and shining. Each of them had pink wings on his back, so

they looked very strange to Jill and Nicky.

"Hi, Dumpy, are you at home?" cried the pixie. The door of the house flew open and a fat gnome with twinkling eyes peeped out.

"Yes, I'm at home," he said. "What can I do for you?"

"These children want to fly to High-Hat's," said the pixie. "But they haven't wings. Could you lend them two of your pigs?"

"Yes, if they'll promise to be kind to them," said Dumpy. "The last time I lent out my pigs someone whipped them and all the curl came out of their tails."

"Oh, these children helped me to take a stone out of my house's shoe," said the pixie, "so I know they're kind. You can trust them. Which pigs can they have, Dumpy?"

"This one and that one," said the fat little gnome, and he drove two plump pigs towards the children. "Catch hold of their tails, children, and jump on their backs. And, whatever you do, speak kindly to them or the curl will come out of their tails."

Jill and Nicky caught hold of the curly tails of the two pigs and jumped on. The pigs' backs were rather slippery but they managed to stay on. Suddenly the fat little animals rose into the air, flapped their pink wings, and flew up the shining rainbow. It was such a funny feeling. The pigs talked to one another in little squeals, and the children were careful to pat them kindly in case the curl came out of their tails.

In ten minutes they came to a towering castle, set right in the middle of the rainbow. It was wreathed in clouds at the top, and was made of a strange black stone that reflected all the rainbow colours in a very lovely manner. It didn't seem a real castle, but it felt real enough when the children touched it. They jumped off the pigs' backs and patted them gratefully.

"Stay here, dear little pigs, till we come out again," said Nicky. Then he and Jill climbed up the long flight of shining

black steps to the door of the castle.
There was a big knocker on it shaped
like a ship. Nicky knocked. The noise
went echoing through the sky just like
thunder, and quite frightened the two
children.

"Come in!" called a deep voice from inside the castle. Nicky pushed open the door and went in. He found himself in a great, high room full of a pale silvery light that looked like moonlight. Sitting at a table, frowning hard, was a giant. He was very, very big, so big that Jill wondered if he could possibly stand upright in the high room. He was sucking a pencil and looking crossly at a book in front of him.

"Good morning," said Nicky politely.

"It isn't a good morning at all," the giant said snappily. "It's a bad morning. One of the very worst. I can't get these sums right again."

"Well, bad morning, then," said Jill. "We've come to ask your help."

"I'm not helping anyone today," growled the giant. "I tell you I can't get these sums right. Go away."

"We must get his help," whispered Nicky to Jill. "We'll keep on trying."

"What sums are they?" Jill asked the giant. To her great surprise High-Hat suddenly picked her up in his great hand

24

and set her by him on the table. When
she had got over her fright Jill looked at
the giant's book.

She nearly laughed out loud when she
saw the sums that were puzzling the
giant. This was one of them: "If two
hens, four dogs and a giant went for a
walk together, how many legs would you
see?"

"I'll tell you the answer to that," she
said. "It's twenty-two!"

The giant turned to the end of the book and looked. "Yes!" he said in astonishment. "You're right! But how did you know that? Do another sum, please."

Jill did all the sums. They were very easy indeed. The giant wrote down the answers in enormous figures, and then sucked his pencil while Jill thought of the next one.

When they were all finished Nicky thought it was time to ask for help again.

"Could you help us now?" he asked. "We've helped you, you know."

"I tell you, this is one of my bad mornings," said the giant crossly. "I never help people on a bad morning. Please go away, and shut the door after you."

Jill and Nicky stared at him in despair. What a nasty giant he was, after all the help they had given him, too! It really was too bad.

"I don't believe you know any magic at all!" said Jill. "You're just a fraud! Why, you couldn't even do easy sums!"

The giant frowned till the children

could scarcely see his big, saucerlike blue eyes. Then he jumped up in a rage and hit his head hard against the ceiling. He sat down again.

"For saying a rude thing like that I will punish you!" he growled in a thunderous voice. "Now listen! You can sit there all year long and ask me to do one thing after another to show you my power – and the first time you can't think of anything I'll turn you into ladybirds!"

Goodness! Jill and Nicky turned quite pale. But in a flash Nicky took the little brown mouse out of his pocket and showed it to the giant.

"You couldn't possibly turn this mouse into a puppydog, I'm sure!" he cried.

The giant gave a snort and banged his hand on the table. "Homminy, tinkaboo-royillabee, juteray, bong!" he cried, and as soon as the magic words were said, hey presto, the little mouse grew bigger and bigger and bigger, and there was Puppydog Pincher again, as large as life, and full of joy at being able to run and jump again. But the giant left the children no time to be glad.

"Next thing, please!" he cried.

"Go to the moon and back!" cried Jill suddenly. In a second High-Hat had vanished completely.

28

"Quick, he's gone to the moon!" cried Jill. "Come on, Nicky, we'll escape before he comes back!"

Out of the castle door they ran, Pincher scampering after them. The two pigs were patiently waiting outside on the rainbow at the bottom of the castle steps. Jill and Nicky jumped on their backs, Nicky carrying the puppy in his arms. Then the flying pigs rose quickly into the air and flew back to the end of the rainbow.

Just as they got there they heard a tremendous noise far up in the air.

"It's the giant, come back from the moon!" said Jill. "Goodness, what a noise he's making! It sounds like a thunderstorm."

The pixie came running to meet them.

"Is that High-Hat making all that noise?" she asked, looking frightened. "Give the pigs back to Dumpy, and climb into my house again with me. The next thing that happens will be High-Hat sliding down the rainbow after you, and we'd better be gone before he arrives.

29

He'll be in a dreadful temper!"

The pigs were given back to the twinkling gnome, and then the children climbed into the walking house with the pixie and Pincher. Off they went at a great rate, far faster than before. Pincher couldn't understand it. He began to bark and that annoyed the grandfather clock very much. It suddenly came out of its corner and boxed Pincher's ears.

"I'm so sorry," said the pixie. "It's a very bad-mannered clock. I only keep it because it's been in my family for so many years. By the way, where do you want to go to?"

"Oh, home, please!" begged the children.

"Right!" said the pixie. Just as she said that there came the sound of a most tremendous bump, and the whole earth shook and shivered.

"There! That's the giant – he's just slid down the rainbow!" said the pixie. "I knew he would bump himself."

The house went on and on. When it came to a sunshiny stretch of road it

skipped as if it were happy. Then the children had to sit down on the bench that ran round the walls and hold tight. Pincher was quite quiet, and he kept looking at the grandfather clock in a very puzzled way.

"Here you are!" suddenly cried the pixie, opening her door. And sure enough, there they were! They were in their very own garden at home, and staring at them in the very greatest astonishment was the gardener, who had never in all his life before seen a house with legs.

The children jumped out and turned to call Pincher, who was barking in excitement. The grandfather clock suddenly ran out of its corner and smacked him as he went.

"Oh, dear, I'm so sorry!" cried the pixie. "It hasn't any manners at all, I'm afraid. Well, see you another day! Goodbye, goodbye!"

The little house ran off, and the children watched it go. What an adventure they had had! And thank goodness Pincher wasn't a mouse any longer but a jolly, jumping puppydog!

"Come on, Pincher!" cried Nicky. "Come and tell Mummy all about your great adventure!"

Off they went and dear me, Mother *was* surprised to hear their strange and exciting story!

She Couldn't
Be Bothered

Do you know anyone who just can't be bothered to do things? You know – they rush out without shutting the door – they won't wipe their feet when they come in – they just can't be bothered to pick up things they drop.

Well, Eileen was just like that. "I can't be bothered," she said to herself a dozen times a day, when she had forgotten to shut the garden gate after her, or had dropped some food on the floor and didn't pick it up. "I can't be bothered."

Now, one day Eileen thought she would have her friends to a little tea party, and they would play at shops. So she bought some tiny sweets, a bag of little biscuits, some chocolate which she broke up into small pieces, some barley-sugar, and a bag of potato crisps, which she loved.

She made a small counter and put her scales there. She got some paper and made some little paper bags. She found her play money and put it into the drawer. She made out some little bills ready for her customers.

"It will be fun to play shop," she thought. "I can be the shopkeeper first and sell all the things. I can weigh them and put them into the bags and make out the bills. Then John and Ken and Mary can have a turn too."

She set out all her goods. They did look

nice. "We can eat them all afterwards," thought Eileen. "They will be lovely."

Soon her friends came along. They looked at the shop Eileen had made and thought it would be good fun.

"I shall like buying such nice things," said John. "I shall buy potato crisps and chocolate."

"I shall buy biscuits," said Ken.

"I shall buy all the barley-sugar," said Mary.

They went in to tea, and sat down at their places. Mother spoke to Eileen.

"Go and shut the door, Eileen. You must have left it open. There really is a very cold wind coming into the room."

"Oh, Mummy, I can't be bothered!" said Eileen, spreading plum jam on her bread-and-butter. "I'm sure I shut it when I let Ken in."

"Well then, you must have left the window open," said her mother. "You'd better go and look."

"Mummy, I really can't be bothered," said Eileen crossly. "I'm quite sure I shut it."

Mother said no more, but helped Mary to spread honey on her bread. If Eileen's guests had not been there she would have made Eileen go and see if the door and window were shut, but she did not want to make a fuss when there were people to tea. So nothing was done.

But as you can guess, Eileen, as usual, had left the door open – and the window of the front room too. And what do you think happened?

Why, two small sparrows hopped on to the windowsill and saw the biscuits so neatly arranged on the counter. And what did they do but hop in and help themselves! They pecked away at those biscuits, and chirruped for joy. Then in came some more sparrows and pecked at the biscuits too.

They all made such a noise that Tibby the cat heard them. Tibby jumped in at the window at once – and when she saw all the sparrows in the front room she was delighted. She pounced on them and they flew in fright round the room. Tibby smelled the potato crisps and gobbled

some of them up. She was very fond of them.

Then she chased those poor birds, who simply could not seem to find the window. They flew round and round the room, squawking with fright. Tibby jumped up on to the counter and knocked everything off – sweets, biscuits, chocolate, everything. It all fell clattering to the floor.

Now Bonzo, Eileen's dog, who was supposed to be in the garden because of his dirty feet, heard all the noise in the front room and tried to see in at the window to find out what was happening. But he couldn't, because the windowsill was too high.

So he wandered round the house to see if a door had been left open – and, of course, he found the front door open wide. Good! In he crept and went to the front room. He chased the cat all over the place, and she tried to jump on to the top of the clock. Over went the clock, *crash*! Goodness, what a noise it made!

Then Bonzo found all the goodies on the floor and he gobbled them up at once – chocolate, barley-sugar, crisps, and the rest of the biscuits.

The cat sat on the mantelpiece and yowled loudly. The sparrows flew wildly round the room. Bonzo gobbled fast. And in the middle of all this Eileen and her mother came in to see what in the world could be happening.

My goodness! How the two of them stared! Eileen burst into tears at once when she saw everything eaten up. Her

mother stared in dismay at the broken
clock.

"You left the window open after all,
Eileen," she cried angrily. "And however
did Bonzo get in? You must have left the
door open too. You bad girl!"

"Oh, don't scold me, Mummy," wept Eileen. "All my nice biscuits and everything are eaten."

"I shall scold you!" said her mother. "Look what's happened because you just couldn't bother yourself to do something. You will have to pay for the broken clock out of your own money."

Well, it was a sad tea party after that. The sparrows flew out of the window when Mother opened it wide. Tibby went to her basket in the kitchen. Bonzo was sent to his kennel. It was no use playing shops because the creatures had eaten everything. So the children played Ludo, and poor Eileen lost every time.

And now she has to pay for the clock. I rather think she'll bother to do things herself in the future, don't you?

The Tale of
Twisty and Ho-Ho

Once upon a time Ho-Ho the goblin went along by the fields to catch the bus that went to the market. He walked by the stream, and sang as he walked, for it was a very pleasant day.

Ho-Ho was going to buy some cows for his master. He was to bring them home that evening. He had cut himself a big stick from the hedge, and with this he meant to drive the cows home. Ah, Ho-Ho felt very important today! He stood still for a moment and looked at the bubbling stream.

"The cows shall drink out of this stream," he said. "They will be thirsty, walking all the way home this hot day."

Now, as Ho-Ho stood watching the sparkling water, he heard the sound of

41

someone whistling, and he turned round to see who was coming. He saw Twisty the gnome coming along, swinging a big stick as he went.

"Good morning, Twisty!" called Ho-Ho. "Where are you going?"

"I'm going to the market to buy my master some sheep," said Twisty, "and this is the stick I have cut to drive them home!"

"Now that is a funny thing!" cried Ho-Ho. "I am going to the market to buy my master some good cows that will be sold there today. And I have cut this stick to drive them home! We will catch the bus together, buy our animals together, and come home together!"

"Yes," said Twisty. "And my master said to me, 'Twisty,' he said, ' see that you give the sheep a drink on the way home, for they will be very thirsty walking so far on the dusty roads.' And when I saw this stream I thought to myself that this should be where they drank."

"No," said Ho-Ho at once. "They cannot drink here, Twisty."

"And why not?" asked Twisty.

"Because my cows will drink here tonight," said Ho-Ho. "And they will be very thirsty indeed, and will drink so much that there will be none left for your sheep."

"Then you must take your cows somewhere else to drink," said Twisty. "For certainly my sheep will drink here! I will not have your cows drinking from this stream for, if they do, there will not be enough water for my sheep!"

"I tell you your sheep shall not drink here!" shouted Ho-Ho.

"And I tell you that your cows shall not drink here!" Twisty shouted back.

Ho-Ho banged his stick on the ground and the dust flew up. "If you bring your sheep to this field, and let them drink from this stream, I shall drive them away," he said.

Twisty hammered his stick on the ground, and the dust flew up in such a cloud that Ho-Ho began to choke. "I tell you, Ho-Ho, if you bring your cows here tonight I shall push them all into the water!" shouted Twisty.

"Indeed you will not!" yelled Ho-Ho. "If you do, I shall hit you with my stick – like that!"

With that he struck Twisty with his stick, and the gnome howled with pain. He lifted his own stick and hit out at Ho-Ho. He knocked his hat off and it fell into the water.

"There goes my best hat!" groaned Ho-Ho and he stamped on the ground in rage. He poked Twisty hard with his

44

stick, and the gnome overbalanced and fell *splash* into the stream!

He sat up in the water and shook his fist at Ho-Ho, who was standing on the bank laughing loudly. Out of the water jumped Twisty, shook himself like a dog, and jumped at Ho-Ho. Over and over on the grass they rolled, and at last down the bank of the stream they went together, *splish-splash*, into the water. How they choked and spluttered as they lay in the water, trying to get out!

"I've swallowed a fish!" said Twisty.

"I've swallowed two!" said Ho-Ho. "And see how wet I am!"

"So am I," said Twisty. "Let us get out and dry our clothes before we go to market. It will never do to go to market dripping wet."

So they climbed out of the stream and sat on the grass in the sun. They took off their coats and hung them on a tree near by to dry.

And, as they sat there, drying, they heard on the road not far off the *rumble – rumble – rumble* of the bus! It was on its way to market, the only bus of the morning!

"The bus! The bus!" shouted Twisty, and he jumped to his feet. "Come quickly, Ho-Ho, or we shall lose it."

They tore off over the field and came to the gate as the bus passed. It stopped when the driver saw them, and the two ran to it – but even as they took hold of the rail to pull themselves into the bus they remembered something!

Their coats! They had left them drying

on the tree; and in the pockets of their coats was the money their masters had given them to buy the cows and the sheep! They could not go to market to buy without money.

"Wait a moment for us," begged Twisty. "We have left our coats in the field."

The gnome and the goblin raced over

the field and took down their wet coats. They turned to go back to the waiting bus, and Twisty said:

"Well now, just you remember, Ho-Ho – on no account are you to bring your cows here tonight to drink from my sheep's stream!"

"What do you mean!" shouted Ho-Ho. "I told you I had chosen it for my cows, and that you were not to bring your sheep!"

Just as they stood glaring at one another they heard *rumble – rumble – rumble –* and the bus had gone on down the lane! It could not wait any longer, for it was already late. It had gone, and the two quarrellers were left behind!

They stared at the rumbling bus in dismay. It climbed the hill and went over the top. They could not get to market that morning.

"I shall have no cows to bring to the stream to drink," said Ho-Ho, in a small voice, "and my master will be very angry with me."

"And I shall have no sheep to bring to

the stream to drink," said Twisty, "and my master will be so angry with me that I shall have no dinner and no supper."

"Why did we quarrel?" said Ho-Ho. "The stream is big enough to give water to all the sheep and cows in the market!"

"We were selfish!" said Twisty. "We each wanted the whole stream for our animals – and now we have no animals to bring to the stream. It serves us right. Goodbye, Ho-Ho. I am going to tell my master that I have missed the bus."

"Goodbye," said Ho-Ho. "I must go back to the farm, too. Next time we meet, Twisty, we will be more sensible."

But I don't somehow think they will – do you?

It Served
Them Right!

Mr Squabble wanted his wife to make a jam sandwich cake for his tea. "Wouldn't you rather have a cherry cake?" asked Mrs Squabble, who liked cherry cakes better than sponge cakes.

"If I say jam sandwich, I don't mean cherry cake," said Mr Squabble.

So Mrs Squabble made a sponge cake. It was a very nice one, yellow and brown. She made it in two halves and put them on the kitchen table to cool.

"I think I shall put raspberry jam in the middle," she said.

"Oh no. Apricot jam is much nicer," said Mr Squabble at once.

"Now look here, Squabble," said Mrs Squabble, rapping on the table. "Now look here . . ."

"I shan't look here, there, or any-where," said Mr Squabble, holding up his newspaper in front of him. "I tell you I want apricot jam."

"And I tell you I want raspberry," said Mrs Squabble, rapping on the table with her rolling-pin.

"Don't do that," said Mr Squabble, who hated noises.

"Don't do what?" asked Mrs Squabble.

"Don't rap on the table like that," said Mr Squabble. "Oh don't, don't, don't! It makes my head spin."

"Well, maybe if your head spins it will do your brains good," said Mrs Squabble.

"Don't be rude," said Mr Squabble, getting up and looking fierce.

"Sit down, and let me get on with my cooking," said Mrs Squabble. "Now, where's that raspberry jam?"

"Apricot jam, you mean!" said Mr Squabble. "I'll get it. It's on the shelf."

"Raspberry jam I said, and raspberry jam I meant," said Mrs Squabble. She went to the cupboard. She put a jar of raspberry jam on the table at the same

moment as Mr Squabble put a jar of apricot jam. They glared at one another.

Mrs Squabble rapped hard on the table again with her rolling-pin. "Squabble! I mean what I say! This jam sandwich is going to have raspberry jam inside, no matter how often you put the apricot jam on the table."

It was Mr Squabble's turn to rap on the table now. He picked up his jar of jam and rapped with that. *Bang, bang, bang!*

"I tell you that I won't eat anything but an apricot sandwich!" he cried.

"Well, don't then," said his wife. "I'll eat the sandwich myself. You don't need to have any. Stop banging the table like that."

"I shall bang all I like!" shouted Mr Squabble, and he banged so hard that he quite frightened the dog, who was lying quietly under the table.

"Well, if you want to bang, two can play at that game!" said Mrs Squabble fiercely, and she took up her rolling-pin again. She banged it on the table – but most unluckily she hit her jar of

raspberry jam. It broke at once and the jam streamed out on to the table, for it was home-made and rather runny.

"Oh! Oh! Look what you've made me do!" cried Mrs Squabble in a rage.

"Good! Very good!" cried Mr Squabble. "Now you will have to use my apricot jam!" He gave the table a good old bang with his jar and he broke the jar in half!

Now it was the turn of the apricot jam to stream out over the table! It began to drip off, and the dog underneath had a most pleasant surprise. He lay there and licked up first a mouthful of raspberry jam and then a mouthful of apricot. He enjoyed it very much.

"You bad man! You've wasted my apricot jam!" wept Mrs Squabble. "Oh, I've a good mind to hit you with this rolling-pin! Oh, I do feel angry!"

She hit the table again – and this time she hit it so hard that the jam sandwich, which still hadn't any jam in it, leaped up into the air, right off the table – and fell gracefully to the floor! One piece broke in half. The dog was delighted and surprised and went to gobble up the broken pieces at once.

"Oh! The sandwich has fallen on the floor!" yelled Mr Squabble, and he tried to get it before the dog could eat it, but unfortunately he trod right on the other half, so that was the end of that. The dog looked up, pleased, and then began to eat the trodden half with great delight. He couldn't understand why Mr and Mrs Squabble were so generous to him all of a sudden.

There was a knock at the door, and Inspector Nosey came in. "I saw you give cake to your dog!" he said sternly. "Don't you know that you should not give animals food like that. And look at him licking up that jam! What! You gave him both raspberry and apricot jam? You must be mad. Pay a fine of five pounds, please, and don't ever do it again."

"We didn't give our dog the sandwich!" cried Mrs Squabble, rapping the table again.

"Mrs Squabble, if you tell stories and rap the table at me, you will have to pay

ten pounds!" said Nosey. "Such waste! I never saw anything like it!"

Mr Squabble paid Inspector Nosey the five pound fine with tears in his eyes. Mrs Squabble cried too.

"Now you can't have a new hat, and I can't have a new armchair," said Mr Squabble sorrowfully, when Inspector Nosey had gone out. "See what quarrelling does for us!"

"And to think that I could have spread one half of the sandwich with raspberry jam and the other half with apricot!" wept Mrs Squabble. "And we could have been sitting down, smiling at one another, eating raspberry-jam sandwich and apricot-jam sandwich together – and now we've lost both jams and the sandwich cake and five pounds! Oh, Squabble, isn't it dreadful! Don't let's quarrel any more!"

"We never will!" said Mr Squabble.

And the dog under the table said, "Wuff-wuffy-wuff-wuff!" which was his way of saying "I don't believe it!" And neither do I!

Peter's Good Luck

One day, when Peter and his friends were racing home from the park, they saw something lying in the gutter. They went up to see what it was. "It's a weight," said Peter, trying to lift it. "It belongs to someone's scales. Perhaps it fell out of Mr Timmins' van when he went round selling his potatoes. My, isn't it heavy!"

"It's a fourteen-pound weight!" said Jim, looking at it. "What shall we do with it? Shall we leave it in the school playground till tomorrow? Then we can play that we are strong men and take it in turns to lift it over our heads, like the man did at the circus last week."

"No, we ought to take it back to Mr Timmins," said Peter. "It doesn't belong to us."

"Finding is keeping," said Harry, trying to lift the weight.

"No, it isn't," said Peter. "You have to find the owner. My mother says so. We must take it back to Mr Timmins."

"What! Carry that heavy weight all the way to the greengrocer's?" said Jim. "You must be mad. And you know what a cross old man Timmins is. He's quite likely to think you're playing a joke on him or something and hit you."

"Come on, Peter, let's drag it into the playground," said Harry. "You surely don't mean to carry it through the village to Mr Timmins' shop."

"Well, won't one of you help me?" asked Peter.

"No thanks!" cried all the boys, and they ran off home, laughing to think of Peter going to the greengrocer's with the heavy fourteen-pound weight.

Peter lifted it on to his shoulder. It was heavy! He went off down the road with it. He didn't want to carry it to Mr Timmins' at all, but he knew that the old greengrocer would want it for his weighing, and would be sorry to have lost it.

"I wish I hadn't seen it now," thought Peter. "It was bad luck, because I really don't want to waste time taking it to that cross old man."

He carried the weight all the way to Mr Timmins' shop, and it seemed heavier and heavier as he went. He was glad when he reached the shop and could put the weight down on the counter.

Mr Timmins wasn't there, but his wife was. She was a nice, plump person with a red face and twinkling eyes. She looked at Peter in surprise.

"Hello, Peter," she said, "what is this?"

"I found it in the road," said Peter. "I thought it might belong to Mr Timmins. I know he uses heavy weights when he weighs out his potatoes."

Mrs Timmins ran her eyes over the weights behind the counter. Then she shook her head. "No," she said, "it isn't ours, Peter. I've got the fourteen-pounder down here. Poor old son! I'm sorry you've had to carry it all this way for nothing. You look quite tired out. I'm just going to sit down to my tea. You come along in and have a piece of my new chocolate cake. I only made it this morning."

Peter was delighted. Chocolate cake was his favourite. He followed Mrs Timmins into her parlour at the back of the shop, and saw the table laid for tea.

"Sit down," said Mrs Timmins.

"Oh, I don't think I ought to stop for long," said Peter. "May I just have a piece of that lovely cake?"

So Mrs Timmins cut him a piece – and a very big slice it was too – and gave it to him. He sat at the table, munching it,

and how he enjoyed it! It was the nicest cake he had ever tasted!

"Thank you very much," he said, when he had finished it. "Now I must go. I suppose I had better take the weight with me. I wonder who it belongs to."

"It could be old Mr Lumkins, the grocer, who dropped it out of his van," said Mrs Timmins. "He keeps his scales too near the back, I always think."

"Well, that's not very far away. I'll take it there," said Peter. So off he went again, the weight on his shoulder. It certainly was very heavy, and his shoulder began to feel tired. But he arrived at last at Mr Lumkins', and put the weight down on

the counter. Mrs Lumkins was behind piles of sugar, biscuit tins and jam-jars, knitting. She was surprised to see Peter.

"What's that you've brought?" she asked, peering over her glasses at the weight.

"Oh, isn't it yours?" said Peter, rather disappointed. "It's a fourteen-pound weight I found in the road. I took it to Mr Timmins' shop first, but it isn't his."

"No, I've got our heavy weights here, all of them," said Mrs Lumkins. "Poor Peter! It's a heavy load to carry about on that small shoulder of yours. Sit down and take a rest. Look, I've just been sorting out some broken biscuits from my biscuit tins. They are in that box. Help yourself. I like to see a boy like you picking up something in the street and doing his best to find the right owner."

"Thank you very much," said Peter, "but I've just had a big piece of chocolate cake at Mrs Timmins', and I feel rather full up. I don't think I can manage a biscuit."

"It must have been a large piece of cake!" said Mrs Lumkins. "Well, here's a paper bag. Fill it with biscuits and take them home with you. You'll be able to eat them sometime, I'm sure! Now, fill it right up to the top. It's a pleasure to give anything to a boy like you!"

Peter went red with pleasure. He filled the paper bag to the top and stuffed it into his pocket. Then he picked up the weight and turned to go.

"I wish I knew whose this weight was," he said. "I can't think of anyone else."

"It looks quite a new one to me," said Mrs Lumkins. "If you took it to Jones, the ironmonger's, he could tell you whose it was, I expect. I dare say it fell out of his van when he was doing his rounds. He might have been taking it to someone who had ordered it."

"Well, I'll take it there," said Peter, and off he went. This time the weight felt heavier than ever, for he really had carried it rather a long way now. He staggered along, wishing that Mr Jones' shop was not quite so far away. He had to sit down and rest a little while before he reached it, but at last he got there. He walked into the shop, put the weight down with a bump on the counter and sank on to a chair, really quite out of breath.

Mr Jones looked at Peter in surprise – then he picked up the weight.

"Hello!" he said, in delight. "Where did you get this? That stupid boy of mine dropped it this morning, and it was a special order for the Red House. Captain Page wanted it today for something important. My word, I'm glad to see it! The captain has been in for it already, and a rare temper he was in when he found out that Fred had dropped it."

"Well," said Peter, "I'm very glad it's yours. Do you know, I've been to Mrs Timmins, and it wasn't hers. And I've been to Mrs Lumkins, and it wasn't hers."

"Do you mean to say you've carried the weight all that distance!" cried Mr Jones, in surprise. "I don't know any other boy who would have troubled himself to find the owner, especially if it

meant carrying such a weight about. Why, most boys would have dragged it off somewhere to play with. Look here, Peter, you come to me whenever you want a job, and I'll give you one. See? I'd like a boy like you. A nice honest boy who'll take a bit of trouble over things. You come to me in the holidays and I'll give you a job and pay you well. Will you do that?"

"Oh, I'd like to," said Peter, full of delight. "My dad is out of work, and I'd like to earn a little money to give to my mother."

"Then you come along to me," said Mr Jones, beaming. "And when you leave school, if you've worked well, I'll take you on here. I want to retire someday, you know, and leave my business to a hard-working young man to manage. Fred's no good. Half asleep most of the time, and always losing things."

Peter could hardly believe his ears. A job for the holidays – and a job when he left school! When it was so hard to get work too! What luck!

"Oh, thank you, sir, you're very kind," he said. "Shall I take this weight to Captain Page's as I go home? It's on my way."

"Do," said Mr Jones. "I'd be grateful if you would. That big lump of a Fred is out somewhere and goodness knows when he'll be back. I can't leave the shop, or I'd go myself. Thanks, my boy. Now, off you go – and don't forget to come along to me in a week's time when the schools break up."

"Thank you, sir," said Peter, and he took the weight on his shoulder again. It

didn't seem at all heavy this time, because Peter was so happy. He felt almost as if he could run with it. He soon came to the Red House and saw Captain Page standing in the garden.

"I've brought the weight you wanted, sir," said Peter, and handed it over.

"Why didn't you bring it sooner, you lazy rascal?" said the captain. "Mr Jones said you had gone out with it a long time ago. You want to hurry up a bit!"

"I'm not Mr Jones's boy," said Peter, feeling rather frightened when he saw how fierce the captain looked. "I just told Mr Jones I'd bring it along for you on my way home. His boy dropped it on his rounds this morning, and I found it."

"Dear me, I beg your pardon," said the captain. "I shouldn't have gone for you like that if I'd known you were doing a kindness. I'm much obliged to you for bringing it along for me. Here's something for your trouble!"

He gave Peter a pound. A whole pound! Peter couldn't believe his eyes.

"Thank you very much, sir," he said.

"It's very generous of you."

He ran all the way home, full of joy.
To think of the luck that heavy weight
had brought him! He gave his mother
the pound and told her the whole story.
She was so proud when she heard it all.

Next day Peter took the bag of biscuits with him and shared them with the other boys. They began to tease him about the weight he had carried away the day before.

"I guess you were sorry you thought you would try to find out who that weight belonged to!" said Jim.

"Well, I'm not sorry at all!" said Peter. "It brought me a large piece of chocolate cake, these biscuits we're eating, the

72

promise of a job in the holidays and a whole pound! What do you think of that?"

"Tell us about it," begged the boys. So Peter told them, and they all listened.

"So, instead of being bad luck to find that heavy weight and carry it all that way, it was the best piece of luck I ever had!" said Peter.

"Next time we find anything we'll do the same as you!" cried the boys.

I wonder if they did, don't you? But you should see Peter now! He is nineteen years old, and manages Mr Jones' shop for him – and all because he once carried a fourteen-pound weight when he was a small boy!

It Was
the Wind!

Tricky and Dob lived next door to one another. Dob was a hard-working little fellow, always busy about something. Tricky was a scamp, and he teased the life out of poor old Dob.

He undid the clothes from Dob's washing-line so that they dropped into the mud. He crept through a hole in his fence and took the eggs that Feathers, Dob's white hen, laid for him. He borrowed this and he borrowed that – but he always forgot to return anything.

Dob put up with Tricky and his ways very patiently, but he did wish Tricky didn't live next to him! He didn't like Tricky at all, but he didn't tell tales or complain about him, so nobody ever punished Tricky or scolded him.

Still, things can't go on like that for ever, and one day a very funny thing happened. It was an autumn day, and the leaves had blown down from the trees, spreading all over Dob's garden. They were making Tricky's garden untidy, too, of course, but he didn't mind a bit. Dob did mind. He was a good little gardener and he loved his garden to be tidy and neat.

So he took his broom and began to sweep his leaves into a big heap. He swept them up by the fence between his garden and Tricky's. There! Now his

garden was tidy again. Dob went to fetch his barrow to put the leaves into it to take down to the rubbish heap.

Tricky had been watching Dob sweeping up his leaves. He grinned. Dob had put the pile of leaves just by the hole in the fence! Tricky slipped out as soon as Dob had gone to fetch his barrow, and went to his fence.

He wriggled through the hole into the middle of the pile of leaves. Then he scattered all the leaves over the grass, and crept back unseen through the hole.

"Dob will be surprised!" he thought. And Dob was. He was annoyed as well. What had happened? A minute ago the leaves had been in a neat pile – now they were all over the place again!

He saw Tricky looking over the fence. "Good-day, Dob," said Tricky, politely. "It's a pity the wind blew your leaves away just as you got them into a pile, wasn't it?"

"The wind?" said Dob, puzzled. "But there isn't any wind."

"Well, it must have been a sudden

mischievous breeze, then," said Tricky, grinning. "You know – a little young wind that doesn't know any better."

"Hmm!" said Dob, and he swept up all his leaves into a pile again. It was lunch-time then, so he left them and went indoors. But he didn't get his lunch at once. He just watched behind his curtain to see if that tiresome Tricky came into his garden to kick away his pile of leaves.

Well, he didn't see Tricky, of course, because that mischievous fellow had wriggled through the hole in the fence which was well hidden by the pile of leaves. He was now in the very middle of the pile – and to Dob's enormous surprise the leaves suddenly shot up into the air, and flew all over the grass.

"What a very peculiar thing!" said Dob, astonished. "I've never seen leaves behave like that before. Can it be that Tricky is right, and that a little breeze is playing about with them?"

He thought about it while he ate his lunch. It couldn't be Tricky, because Dob hadn't seen him climb over the fence and go to the pile. One minute the pile had been there, neat and tidy – and the next it had been scattered all over the place.

"I'll sweep up the leaves once more," thought Dob. "And I'll put them into my barrow before that wind gets them again."

But of course Tricky got into the next pile, too, through the hole in the fence, and Dob found his leaves scattering all round him. He was very cross and very puzzled.

Soon Tricky called to him. He had wriggled out of the pile, through the hole in the fence and was now back in his own garden, grinning away at Dob.

"My word – are you still sweeping up

leaves? There's no end to it, Dob."

"I think you must have been right when you said that the wind is playing tricks with me," said Dob. "But the thing is, what am I to do about it?"

"Catch the bad fellow and make him prisoner!" said Tricky.

"But how can you catch the wind?" asked Dob.

"Well, haven't you seen how the wind loves to billow out a sail, or blow out a sack or a balloon?" said Tricky. "Just get a sack, Dob, put the wind in it when he next comes along, tie up the neck and send him off by carrier to the Weather-Man to deal with. He'll give him a spanking, you may be sure!"

"Well – if I could catch the wind that way I would certainly do all you say," said Dob. "But I'm afraid it isn't possible."

All the same, he went and got a sack and put it ready nearby in case the wind did come along again. Tricky watched him sweep up his leaves once more, and he simply couldn't resist creeping through the hole to play the same trick on poor old Dob again!

But this time Dob was on the watch for the wind, and as soon as he saw the leaves just beginning to stir, he clapped the sack over the pile. He felt something wriggling in the leaves, and gave a shout. "I've got him! I've caught the wind! He's filling up my sack! Aha, you scamp of a wind, I've got you!"

Tricky wriggled and shouted in the sack, but Dob shook him well down to the bottom of it, together with dozens of leaves, and tied up the neck firmly with rope.

"It's no good wriggling and shouting like that!" he said, sternly. "You're caught. It's a good thing Tricky told me how to catch you! Now, off to the Weather-Man you're going, and goodness knows what he'll do with you!"

He wrote a big label:

To be delivered to the Weather-Man by the carrier – one small, mischievous breeze. Suggest it should be well spanked before it is allowed to blow again.

And when the carrier came by with his cart, Dob handed the whimpering Tricky to him, tightly tied up in the sack. The carrier read the label and grinned.

"I'll deliver him all right," he said. "The Weather-Man isn't in a very good temper lately – I'm afraid he will spank this little breeze hard."

Dob went to look over the fence to find

Tricky and tell him that his good idea
had been carried out – but Tricky was
nowhere to be seen, of course! And he
was nowhere to be seen for three whole
days! Dob was very puzzled.

He came back the evening of the third
day. He looked very solemn indeed. The
Weather-Man had spanked him well and
truly, and had set him to do all kinds of
blowing jobs, which made Tricky very
much out of breath.

"Hello, Tricky! Wherever have you
been?" cried Dob.

Tricky wouldn't tell him. He wouldn't

tell anyone. But everyone agreed that his three days away had done him good – he wasn't nearly so mischievous, and ever since that day he has never played a single trick on old Dob.

"I can't imagine why!" said Dob. How he would laugh if he knew!

Chack-
Chack-Chack!

One day, when Micky and Pam were walking along the lane that ran round the great hill on which the old ruined castle stood, they heard, as usual, the clacking and chacking of the hundreds of jackdaws there.

They stood and looked at the birds flying round and about the towers of the castle. What a number there were! And what a noise they made. *Chack, chack, chack, chack!*

"They build their nests in the tops of those towers," Micky told Pam. "They fill them up with hundreds of twigs and then nest on the top of them."

"I know," said Pam. "I always thought they were rooks till you told me they were jackdaws."

"Rooks are larger birds," said Micky. "Anyway, you can always tell a jackdaw, if he is close to you, because the back of his neck is grey, not black. Look – there's one down in the lane, see – after that bit of bread."

Pam looked – and yes, she could see the grey patch at the nape of his neck quite well. And then, as she was still standing watching the jackdaw, a big cat leaped straight out of the hedge on top of him.

The jackdaw tried to fly off in fright – but one of the paws of the cat caught his wing, and the claws prevented him from getting away. The cat pulled the bird down to the ground and attacked it.

Pam gave a scream, and Micky shouted and ran to the struggling bird, who was crying "Chack, chack, chack" at the top of his voice.

It was very difficult to rescue the frightened bird, and before he had managed to get it away from the cat, Micky's hands were covered with scratches. The cat was half wild, a stray

who lived by hunting. He slunk away angrily, feeling that he had been unfairly cheated of a meal.

"Poor thing!" said Pam, almost in tears as she looked at the panting bird. "Will it die? Look at its poor wing – it's limp and bleeding."

"It does look pretty bad," said Micky. "Let's take it home to Mum. She'll know what to do. She always does."

So they carried the scared, bleeding bird home, and their mother came running as soon as she saw them carrying it in.

"Don't let little Timmy see it!" she said. "It would scare him. Bring it in here."

Timmy was their baby brother. He was playing happily in the next room, and he knew nothing of the hurt jackdaw, though he wondered what the sudden *chack-chack-chack* noise was that it made when Mother bathed its hurt wing.

They put the injured bird into a box and Mother carried it to an airy cupboard. "It needs darkness and quiet,"

she said. "It's a young bird, not an old one, so it may have enough health and strength to recover."

"But what about food?" said Pam. "It will be hungry."

"Well, see if you can find some slugs or grubs in the garden," said Mother. "That will be helping Daddy and the young jackdaw at the same time."

Before three days had gone by, the jackdaw was bright and talkative. Mother had brought it into the sitting-room so that it might have company. It couldn't walk, for both its legs had been injured, and its right wing was still limp and useless.

Timmy was most surprised to see it. "Dicky-bird!" he said, and tried to stroke its black head.

"Mind it doesn't peck you!" said Mother. But the jackdaw never once pecked the little boy, no matter how he fussed over it, either then or in the days that followed.

"It seems to like Timmy better than any of us," complained Pam. "It always begins to talk when he comes into the room."

The jackdaw's legs grew better, and one day he stretched out his injured wing as well as his whole one. "Look! That one's all right now too!" said Micky, in delight.

"He'll fly away soon," said Mother.

"No," said Timmy, at once. "I want him. He is my Chack-Chack."

"He's *ours*," said Micky.

But there was no doubt about it – Chack-Chack, as everyone now called

him, was much more Timmy's than anyone else's. When the jackdaw was put into the garden, he followed the little two-year-old all over the place.

He could fly now – but he didn't fly away back to his friends. No – he liked this family. He liked having the scraps given to him at the kitchen door. He sometimes took a little flight and had a talk with the older jackdaws, but always he came back.

Timmy didn't like him to fly away. He welcomed him back with cries of "Chack-

Chack! Here's Chack-Chack, Mummy!" And there the jackdaw would be, sitting on his shoulder, rubbing his black-feathered head against Timmy's cheek.

"It looks as if we've got that bird for ever," said Daddy. "I wish you'd keep him out of the house, though – I've missed a pair of cufflinks and my tiepin lately and I'm pretty certain Chack-Chack has taken them."

"Oh dear! I'm sorry," said Mother. "Jackdaws do so like bright things. I'll try to keep him out of the house."

But that wasn't easy – especially as the jackdaw discovered that by coming to a shut door and knocking hard on it with his beak, somebody usually opened it!

Granny always opened the back door when he knocked, and gave him some scraps. Timmy always opened the garden door when he heard the familiar *knocka-knocka-knock* of the bird's strong, hard beak – and dear me, Mother often opened the front door to him, because his beak chipped off the paint and she didn't want him to do that!

He really was a very clever bird – but oh, so mischievous. He undid everyone's shoelaces under the table. He went off with Mother's silver pencil and nobody could find it. He took Pam's silver chain, and Micky's nails from his carpentry set. He hid them in all sorts of places!

Mother was quite glad when she could

send Timmy and the jackdaw out into the garden together. At least Timmy kept him out of mischief. Really, Chack-Chack was like a fourth child to be looked after! Timmy loved going with him. He and Chack-Chack walked solemnly all round the garden together, and examined every corner every day.

But they never went through the little locked gate in one corner. That led to Mother's special rose-garden, a dear little place with crazy paving and rose-beds and a lily pond in the middle. It was kept locked because Mother didn't want it spoilt, and because she was afraid that Timmy might wander there and fall into the pond.

Timmy and Chack-Chack looked at the pond every day through the little wrought-iron gate. Sometimes a goldfish jumped out of the pond after a fly. Sometimes a thrush came down and sent silver drops all over the place. Timmy always wished he was big enough to go into the little rose-garden, but Mother said no, not till he was a big boy of five.

One day Chack-Chack was really very naughty. He was hungry, so he went to knock with his beak on the back door. Nobody answered it. He went to the garden door and did the same thing. Then he went to the front door and knocked so hard that he chipped off quite a little pile of paint.

Mother and Granny were busy upstairs, and they really couldn't bother to go down to Chack-Chack. So after a time he decided to get in another way. He hadn't learned about windows yet, because whenever he flew on to a sill, the window was shut at the bottom, and the jackdaw wasn't clever enough to look and see if he could get in at the top.

This morning the kitchen window was open at the bottom when he flew on to the sill – so in he went, highly delighted. Ah – he had the kitchen all to himself!

He pecked the nice new cake on the table. He upset a jug of milk. He pecked the flowers off all Granny's geranium plants in the window. Then he hopped down to the floor and walked into the living-room.

What a time he had! He flew up on Father's desk and pecked the papers

there to pieces. He flew off with a pen and dropped it behind the settee. He tugged at a flower and upset the vase it was in. He found a necklace Pam had been threading and broke it, so that all the beads fell on the floor.

He certainly got into trouble! Father was very angry about his spoilt papers, and Granny was so upset over her spoilt geraniums that she cried.

"That's the end!" said Father. "Chack-Chack will have to go. It's time he went and joined his friends, anyway – he's a grown bird now. I'll take him off to the castle tomorrow, set him free, and you'll see – he won't come back."

"No," said Timmy, quite fiercely. "NO. I want Chack-Chack."

But when Father said a thing he meant it, and next afternoon he and Pam and Micky took the jackdaw in a closed basket to the castle where he had been born. They set him free and he swooped up into the air joyously to greet all the other birds. They flew round him in excitement, chattering loudly.

"Goodbye, Chack-Chack!" called Pam. "Have a good time. Come back and see us whenever you like."

Timmy was very sad. He missed Chack-Chack badly that day. Next day he went to look for him in the garden, but the jackdaw wasn't there. He was having a wonderful time with his friends, flying high in the air, calling loudly, and going for long flights with all his family.

But that afternoon he remembered the nice family he had lived with. He especially remembered Timmy. He wanted to see him and play with him. He wanted to hear the little boy calling him: "Chack-Chack, where are you?"

So the jackdaw left the big castle and flew back to the home he knew so well. Timmy would be in the garden. He always played in the garden till teatime.

The jackdaw flew down into the garden but Timmy was not there. The bird looked all round, flying here and there to look for Timmy. And then he saw him.

Timmy was in the rose-garden! He had looked over the gate as usual, and had seen a goldfish jump so far out of the pond that it had landed on the nearby grass, and there it was wriggling and struggling, panting for breath, trying to get back to the water.

Timmy had climbed right over the gate. It was locked, so he couldn't open it, but somehow, somehow, he had to save that silly little goldfish. So over the gate he climbed, and into the rose-garden.

He picked up the goldfish and went to the edge of the pond with it. He let the fish slide in and swim away. Then he saw a yellow waterlily, and reached out to touch it – and *splash*! into the water he went!

The jackdaw saw him and flew into the little rose-garden. "Chack-chack-chack!" he called excitedly. But Timmy didn't answer. Timmy was struggling in the deep little pond, and he couldn't get out.

The jackdaw was frightened. He pecked at Timmy's foot, but Timmy took no notice. "Chack!" said the jackdaw solemnly, and then flew off to the house.

He hammered at the back door with his strong beak. He hammered and hammered, more loudly and quickly than he had ever done before! Mother heard him and came at once.

"Why, it's Chack-Chack back again!" she said, and then stared in astonishment as he caught the end of her skirt in his beak and pulled hard at it. "Let go, now, you bad bird, let go!"

But Chack-Chack wouldn't let go, and Mother suddenly knew that he wanted her to go with him. She cast a quick look round the garden. Where was Timmy? Why wasn't he with the jackdaw he liked so much?

The jackdaw tugged and tugged and led her at a run to the little iron gate. She saw at once what had happened and gave a scream. Like Timmy, she climbed over the gate. She ran to the struggling child and dragged him out of the water, choking and spluttering.

Mother knew what to do. She held him

upside down first of all, and then she laid him on the grass. Would she have to get him breathing properly? She knew how to do that. But no – after some more choking and spluttering Timmy sat up, gasping.

"Chack-Chack!" he choked, and the jackdaw flew on to his shoulder at once. Mother wiped the little boy's face.

"If it hadn't been for old Chack-Chack coming hammering at the door to tell me you were in the pond, goodness knows what would have happened!" she said, taking Timmy into her arms and carrying him indoors. "Come on, Chack-Chack – you shall have the finest meal you have ever had in your life!"

Well, after that, of course, there was never anything said about Chack-Chack being a nuisance and having to go away.

"Take all my silver pencils, my cufflinks and tiepins if you like – but stay, Chack-Chack, stay!" said Father. And everyone said the same.

So the jackdaw is still there. You'd love to see him – but do be careful that he doesn't pull both your shoelaces undone!

The Very
Clever Kite

Timothy was so excited. His mother was going to take him to see a conjurer at the Town Hall, and it was said that he could really do the most marvellous things imaginable! He could put water into a teapot, and when it poured out, it was cocoa! And then, by waving his handkerchief over the cup of cocoa, he could turn it into a bowl with a goldfish swimming about. Just imagine that!

So it was no wonder that Timothy was excited. He kept thinking and thinking and thinking about the conjurer, and he was so pleased and happy that he simply could not sit still for a moment!

It was a very windy day. The trees sang a song as they swung their branches about. The smoke from the chimneys twisted this way and that like witches' cloaks, and the flag on the flagpole on the village green flapped as if it had wings!

There came a knock at the door. Mother went to it, and there was the milkman with the three bottles of milk.

"Wait a moment," said Mother. "I will pay you."

She ran to get her bag, and took a twenty-pound note out of it. Just as she was handing it to the milkman, a dreadful thing happened. The wind suddenly blew by in a terrific gust and snatched the note out of Mother's hand.

It was blown away, high in the air, and flew right over the hedge and was lost to sight!

"Oh no!" cried Mother, in dismay. "Quick! Let's look for it! Timothy! Come and help!"

Well, they all hunted and hunted and hunted – but not a sign of that twenty-pound note could they see! It might have blown as far as the next village, for all they knew.

Mother went sadly back to the house.

"Timothy, I can't take you to see the conjurer now," she said. "I am so very sorry. But I've no more money."

Timothy was dreadfully disappointed. He wanted to cry – but when he saw his mother looking so upset he knew that he must pretend not to care, so that she wouldn't feel even more unhappy. So he gave her a hug, and said, "Never mind, Mum! I don't mind about the conjurer! Don't you worry about me!"

Wasn't that nice of him? He went and put on his jacket to go and tell his friend Jimmy that he would not be going to

see the conjurer now, and to ask Jimmy if he would be sure to remember everything to tell him, if he went.

"Jimmy's out in the field flying his kite," said Jimmy's mother. So Timothy ran to the field and sure enough, there was Jimmy, flying his kite high in the air. What a wind there was! The boys could hardly hear themselves speak!

"The kite can't go any higher!" said Jimmy. "I've used every single inch of string!"

"I hope the string won't break," said Timothy anxiously. "The kite is pulling very hard!"

And do you know, just as he spoke, the string did break! Wasn't it dreadful? It broke a little way up in the air – and the kite at once flew away, dragging its long tail and its string behind it!

"Oh!" cried Jimmy, in dismay. "My lovely kite! It's gone!"

The two boys watched it. It dipped down suddenly, then dipped again, and disappeared behind a tree.

"Quick!" said Timothy. "We may get it if we hurry. Perhaps it is caught somewhere."

The boys raced over the field, climbed over the wall at the end, and found themselves in a little wood. They hunted anxiously for the kite, and could not see it anywhere.

"It's too bad!" said Timothy. "This horrid wind! It blew away my mum's money today so that she can't take me to see the conjurer and now it's taken away your kite!"

They went on hunting – and suddenly Timothy gave a shout, and pointed upwards.

"Look! It's up there! Caught in that tree!"

"Oh dear! I can't climb that tree," said Jimmy. "I'd be afraid of falling."

"Well, *I'll* climb it and get the kite," said Timothy. "I'm used to climbing. I'm always climbing the trees in our garden at home."

So up he went. It was very difficult. A branch caught at his leg and scratched it. A big twig stuck into his cheek and pricked him. But up he went – and at last he reached the kite. He pulled it free from the branch it had fallen on, and was just about to go down again when he saw a big hole in the tree. "I wonder if there's a nest there," he thought, and slipped his hand in.

There was a nest – but it was a very old one, falling to pieces. There was something that rustled in the nest. Timothy thought it was a dead leaf. He pulled it out to see.

But when he saw what it was he got such a surprise that he very nearly fell right out of the tree! It was the twenty-pound note his mother had lost! Yes, it was, really!

"The wind must have blown it all the way across the field, into this tree – and it must have slipped into the hole!" cried

Timothy. "Oh Jimmy, Jimmy, what luck! Now Mum will be able to take me to see the conjurer after all. Hurrah!"

"Hurrah!" cried Jimmy too, pleased to see his friend's excited face. "Throw down the kite, Timothy. We'll race home and tell your mother."

They tore off – and Timothy's mother was so pleased and excited. She hugged both little boys, and heard the story of how the kite got caught in the tree, again, and again, and again.

"We'll go to see the conjurer and we'll take Jimmy with us, as it was his kite that so kindly found my money for me!" she laughed.

"Wasn't it a clever kite!" said Jimmy, full of joy to think that he was going to have such a treat.

Well, they all went to see the conjurer that afternoon, and didn't they have fun! Do you know, the conjurer took a pound out of Jimmy's left ear, and a rabbit out of Timothy's cap. It was really most astonishing!

"I don't think I've ever seen a cleverer thing!" cried Jimmy, as they went home.

"Except your kite!" said Timothy. "That was even cleverer than the conjurer, Jimmy! It found a twenty-pound note in a bird's nest instead of an egg!"

The Boy Who
Made Faces

Willie was a very good-looking little boy, and his mother was proud of him. She didn't know how ugly he looked when she wasn't there.

He pulled faces. He made faces to frighten the little girls. He made faces behind the teacher's back at school, just to feel clever. He made faces at other people just to be rude.

He screwed up his nose. He squinted. He blew out his cheeks. And when he wanted to be very rude he put out his tongue. The little girls were really frightened of him, especially when he rolled his eyes round and round and round.

"One day, Willie, the wind will change when you are making a face," said old

Mrs Lambie. "And then your face will get stuck. You are a very rude little boy. I only wish your father knew the rude faces you make at me and at other people you meet."

Willie didn't like Mrs Lambie. He squinted at her and put out his tongue, and then he ran away. He really was a very rude little boy.

"Pooh! Fancy telling me that old story about my face getting stuck if the wind changes," said Willie, and he laughed. "What a lot of nonsense!"

And then something happened. It happened that very afternoon, as Willie was going home from school. He passed the old man who sold newspapers at the corner and, as he always did, he put his tongue out at him. In and out went his tongue, in and out, and Willie danced round as he made his face.

The wind changed suddenly. One moment it was blowing from the west; the next moment it dropped – and then it blew again from the east . . .

And Willie's face was stuck! He squinted and his tongue went in and out! He didn't notice it at first as he ran off squinting, his tongue going in and out rudely.

"Oh, dear – I've squinted too hard and my eyes won't come right," said Willie suddenly. "And why won't my tongue keep in? Goodness, here comes my headmaster. I'd better cross to the other side of the road."

But his headmaster called to him:

"Good afternoon, Willie. Hurry along home."

To Willie's horror his red tongue came out and waggled itself at the Head, who looked most astonished and annoyed. Before he could say a word Willie, as red as a beetroot, tore down the road and disappeared round a corner.

He was beginning to feel very worried. He still couldn't see very well, because his eyes were squinting just as much, and it was very, very difficult for him to keep his tongue in his mouth, even if he dug his teeth into it.

He slipped indoors. His mother called to him. "Willie, you're late! Wash and then come to tea."

Willie washed. He had managed to keep his tongue in his mouth for a little while, but he didn't know how long it would remain tucked inside his mouth. He sidled into the dining-room, not looking at his mother.

He began his tea, and his tongue was soon so busy helping his teeth to eat that Willie forgot about it. He looked at his mother when she spoke to him – and out went his tongue! His mother gazed at him in horror.

"Willie! What are you putting your tongue out at me for? And oh, don't squint like that! Willie, do you hear me? Don't be such a rude, silly little boy!"

But that tongue waggled away, and his mother got up sharply. She took Willie from his chair, and sent him out of the room.

Soon his father came home looking angry. "Where's Willie?" he said. "I met his headmaster when I was out, and he told me that Willie actually made faces at him when he met him in the road. I can't have that. Where is he?"

"He's upstairs," said Willie's mother. "I sent him out of the room for making faces at me. Whatever has come over him?"

"Well, whatever it is, I'll soon change him!" said Willie's father, and he went up to find Willie. The boy heard him coming, and in a panic he got into bed, clothes and all, and pulled the sheet halfway over his face.

"Oh, I hope I don't put my tongue out at Daddy!" he thought. "Oh dear, this is

119

dreadful. I must keep my teeth tightly closed, then my tongue won't come out."

His father came in. "Willie," he said, "what is this I hear from your headmaster? Did you really pull faces at him? Have you gone mad?"

Willie shook his head, not daring to unclose his teeth to speak, in case his tongue popped out.

"Answer me properly, yes or no," said his father angrily. "Shaking your head like that! And what are you squinting for?"

"Oh, Daddy," began poor Willie, but he got no further because out popped his tongue and waggled itself at his astonished father.

Well, quite a lot of things happened to Willie after that, because his father had a hot temper and didn't allow boys to behave rudely to him.

"That's for being rude to your headmaster, to your mother and to me," said his father. "Three very good spanks. Now let me see if your tongue is better."

Well, whether the wind changed again at that moment or not, I don't know, but certainly Willie's tongue behaved itself after that. Maybe it was as frightened as poor Willie! But the dreadful thing was that his eyes didn't come right, and he still squinted.

So now he has to wear glasses till they get right, and he doesn't like it a bit. He does wish he had never pulled such silly faces.

The Little Red Shawl

There was once a little old lady who lived in a tiny cottage and knitted all day long. One day she bought some red wool and it was such a lovely colour that she thought she would make it into a little red shawl.

So she set to work. She knitted hard for many weeks and at last the shawl was finished. It was very beautiful, and there was not a mistake in it.

On the day that it was finished a carriage and pair drove up the road past the little old lady's cottage. In the carriage sat the queen of that land, a lovely lady, and as good as she was beautiful. She wore a pretty dress but no coat, and just as she passed the little old lady's cottage, she sneezed three times.

"Dear me!" she said. "How foolish I was not to wear a coat this afternoon. I know I shall catch a cold!"

Now, the little old lady had very sharp ears and she heard every word that the Queen said. In a second she caught up the little red shawl and ran out into the street. The carriage had just passed, but the old lady called after it:

"Coachman! Coachman! Stop, please!"

The coachman heard her voice and turned his head in surprise. The Queen heard the shouting too, and when she saw that it was a little old lady, she told the coachman to stop and see what was the matter.

So the carriage stopped and the old lady trotted up, all out of breath, but as pleased as punch.

"Your Majesty," she said. "You are cold. Here is a little red shawl that I have just finished making. Please accept it and wear it today in your carriage."

"Thank you very much," said the Queen, and she took it and wrapped it round her shoulders. "How beautifully warm it is! I shall love to wear it. Now do please get into the carriage with me and come and have tea at the palace."

Well, the little old lady could hardly believe her ears! She got her best bonnet and wrap and popped into the carriage beside the Queen. Then off they drove to the palace and the old lady had the time of her life eating jam sandwiches and chocolate cake with the lovely Queen.

The little red shawl was delighted to find itself round the Queen's shoulders. It wrapped her round very warmly and was very proud.

"I shall look after her and keep her from getting cold every day," it thought. "How lucky I am to belong to the Queen!"

The Queen loved the little red shawl. She wore it every evening, and it suited her very well. For five years she kept it and the shawl was very happy for it was well taken care of. It was washed every week, and whenever a tiny hole came in it it was mended carefully. But at the end of five years the Queen looked at it and sighed.

"My dear little shawl," she said, "I am afraid I must part with you. You are really getting too old for me to wear. There are so many thin places in you that soon you will be nothing but holes! I must give you away."

How upset the shawl was to hear that! It looked at itself in the glass and sure enough it looked very old, and certainly not fit to be round the shoulders of the Queen, who was lovelier than ever.

The next week the Queen's old nurse came to stay, and the Queen thought that it would be a good idea to give the shawl to her, for she had nothing but a black wrap that had no warmth in it at all – and even though the little red shawl was old, it was still very warm to the shoulders.

So the old nurse took the shawl and had it for her own. She wore it every day and when she left the palace she took it with her. At first the shawl missed the Queen very much, but it soon became fond of the old nurse. She had many friends who admired the shawl and thought her lucky to have one that the Queen herself had worn.

The shawl was still washed carefully every week and mended. But the old nurse had not got very good eyesight, so the darns were rather ugly, and soon the shawl looked patchy, with darns of pink, blue and green here and there.

Then one day the nurse went to see a woman who had just got a new little baby of her own. The woman was very poor and she had no shawl for the tiny little girl who lay in her cot as good as gold.

"You must have my shawl," said the old nurse. "Take care of it, for the Queen herself gave it to me. Wrap it round the baby and it will keep her beautifully warm."

So once again the shawl changed hands, and became the baby's wrap. Every day the little creature was wrapped warmly in it, and when the shawl felt tiny hands pulling at it it was glad. The baby loved the old shawl, and thought it was a beautiful colour.

The shawl was happy. It liked to be loved, and it always rejoiced when the mother wrapped it tightly round the baby's warm little body. But soon the little girl grew up, and when she was three years old the mother put the shawl into a cupboard and left it hanging there.

It was very dirty for it had only once been washed by the mother, and it was so full of holes that there was no use in mending it. It hung in the cupboard for weeks and weeks, till one day an old beggar-woman came to the door with some plants to sell.

"I don't want any plants," said the mother. "I have no money to spend."

"Now see this beautiful plant, all in blossom," said the beggar-woman. "Have you no old coat or old shawl you could give me? You shall have this plant in exchange."

The mother suddenly remembered the little red shawl hanging in the cupboard, and she ran to fetch it. The shawl felt itself taken down from its peg and it wondered if it was going to wrap the little girl round again. It had been very unhappy and lonely for weeks, for no one had taken any notice of it at all.

"Here you are," said the mother. "You can have this old shawl, if you like. Give me the plant in exchange."

The beggar-woman took the shawl and put it round her shoulders. Then she gave the mother the plant and went off down the path.

The shawl was glad to be round someone again. It hugged the beggar-woman tightly, and she was glad of the warmth. She pulled it more closely round her and the shawl could have sung for joy.

At last someone wanted it again!

For six months, in wind and rain, the beggar-woman wore the shawl. It was soaked with rain, and scorched with the sun, but it was happy because the beggar-woman loved it.

Then one day someone gave the woman a fine coat with a fur collar. She threw off the shawl and put on the coat. How proud she was! She didn't give another thought to the shawl, but went on her way singing. The shawl was left in a ditch, and it lay there unheeded for weeks.

It was very sad. It remembered the days when the Queen had worn it, and thought of all the grand people who had admired it. It thought of the old nurse and how carefully she had washed it each week, just as the Queen had done. It thought of the little baby it had warmed day after day, and last of all it thought of the beggar-woman who had worn it in all weathers.

"Now nobody wants me," sighed the shawl as it lay forgotten in the ditch.

Now, standing in the field nearby was a scarecrow. He wore an old top hat, a ragged coat and a pair of old breeches. He stood out there in the middle of the field, and frightened the crows and jackdaws who came hopping round. He was a merry fellow, and often sang a song as he stood doing his work. He was only made of beansticks with a turnip for a head, but he flapped about in the wind as lively as could be.

One day a tramp came by and saw the old scarecrow standing there, flapping its coat in the wind.

"That coat's better than mine," said the tramp, and he popped into the field, took off the scarecrow's coat and made off with it. Then how funny the old scarecrow looked! He had only a hat and his breeches, and he felt very cold indeed.

He shivered and shook in the wind, for he missed the coat very much. Then he began to sneeze, and he nearly sneezed his turnip head off.

"Oh my, oh my!" he groaned. "I shall catch a dreadful cold, I know I shall!"

The little red shawl peeped through the hedge and saw him. It felt very sorry for the scarecrow, and wished that it was near enough to talk to him. Then suddenly a splendid idea came to the shawl.

"Ho, wind!" said the shawl. "Blow me into the field, please."

So the wind blew the shawl into the field, and it lay there near the scarecrow.

"Oh, little red shawl!" cried the scarecrow. "Come a little nearer! If only you could put yourself round my shoulders, it would be fine."

But the little red shawl couldn't do that, and the wind couldn't seem to manage it either. Then one morning the farmer came into his field and saw that the scarecrow had lost his coat. He spied the shawl nearby and he picked it up and wrapped it round the scarecrow's shoulders.

How happy they both were! The shawl was full of joy to warm someone again, and the scarecrow no longer shivered and shook in the breeze. He was as warm as toast.

"Tell me about your life," said the scarecrow.

Then the shawl began to tell of its adventures, just as they are told to you, and the scarecrow listened in delight.

"But now I am happier than ever before!" said the little red shawl. "I love you, old scarecrow, and I am sure you love me!"

"You are the most beautiful shawl in the world!" said the scarecrow. And the best of it was that the scarecrow really meant what he said!

Poor
Mr Dawdle!

Mr Dawdle was as lazy as his name.

He dawdled all day long! He got up late – he dawdled over his breakfast – he dawdled to his work – and he dawdled home again!

Mrs Dawdle used to get so cross with him.

"Wake up, Dawdle! You're dreaming again! Hurry, hurry!"

But he wouldn't hurry . . . So Mrs Dawdle wrote to his cousin, Mr Hurry-Up, and asked him to invite Mr Dawdle to stay with him. She knew that would cure him all right!

Mr Dawdle was pleased when he got the letter from Hurry-Up, asking him to stay with him.

"That will be a nice rest for me," he

said. "I shall enjoy it. I will go tomorrow. Pack my bag, dear."

So the next day Dawdle caught the bus (only just!) and arrived at the village of Quickmarch where his cousin Hurry-Up lived. What a smart village it was! Everyone so neat and clean, walking about smartly. Every house nicely painted, every garden neat and trim. My word, it was a model village. Hurry-Up lived in a small house, painted blue and yellow, and its knocker shone very brightly indeed.

"Hello, hello, hello!" said Hurry-Up, opening the door to Dawdle. "Pleased to see you, Dawdle. Come in!"

Dawdle went in. The kitchen was neat and tidy. So was Dawdle's bedroom – very neat indeed. Dawdle thought he would never be able to keep it as neat as that!

He spent a very pleasant evening with his cousin, and then went to bed.

"Breakfast at eight o'clock sharp!" said Mr Hurry-Up. "And don't take too long undressing, Dawdle, because candles are expensive here. Hurry yourself!"

Dawdle sat down on his bed. He couldn't possibly hurry himself! Not he! He took off one sock. This took him about ten minutes – and at the end of that time Hurry-Up rushed in, blew out the candle, and said goodnight!

Dawdle was left in the dark! Oh dear! He couldn't see to take off his other sock, for it took him about five minutes to find his foot. He couldn't see to undo his buttons, and how he undid them he really didn't know! At last he was

undressed, and somehow or other got into his pyjamas – though he put his sleeves on his legs and his arms through the trouser part!

Then he tried to find the bed. He walked into the wall three times, and knocked over the washstand. Then he nearly walked out of the window. At last he bumped into the bed and got into it. What a relief! He drew the blankets up and didn't dawdle about going to sleep. No – he was soon snoring loudly.

At seven o'clock in the morning Mr Hurry-Up knocked on the door. "Time to get up, Dawdle!"

Dawdle said "Ooooooph!" and fell asleep again.

At half past seven Hurry-Up knocked again. "Getting up, Dawdle?"

"Oooooph!" said Dawdle, and fell asleep again. At eight o'clock a glorious smell came in to the room – the smell of frying bacon, eggs, and mushrooms, a smell of new-made toast and fresh coffee! It woke Mr Dawdle from his dreams.

A gong sounded through the house. "Dong-a-dong-dong!" There came a crash at his door. It was Mr Hurry-Up on his way to breakfast. "Hurry! Breakfast is ready!"

Dawdle got out of bed. He was hungry – but he was so little used to hurrying that he made the silliest mistakes. He put two socks on one foot. He put his vest over his pyjamas. He forgot to fasten his braces. He put his shirt on back to front. He did his jacket up all wrong. Oh dear!

At last he went down to breakfast.
Only Mrs Hurry-Up was there, looking
very fierce. "You're very late, Dawdle,"
she began – and then she caught sight of
his appearance – only one shoe, curious-
looking shirt, no collar, coat done up
wrong, hair not brushed!

"Look at yourself in the mirror, Dawdle," she said angrily. "Is this the way to come down?"

Dawdle looked at himself and blushed with horror. He fled upstairs and spent twenty minutes putting everything right. Then he came downstairs again.

The breakfast was cleared away and washed up! There wasn't a crumb to eat! Dawdle was so upset – but he didn't dare to ask for any. Just at that minute Hurry-Up came in. "Hello, Dawdle," he said.

"Had a good breakfast? My, weren't those mushrooms good? Hurry up, because we've got to catch the bus to market. It goes in ten minutes' time. We shall get our lunch in the next town. Mr Spickspan has asked us to go to his house."

Dawdle went to find his pipe. He couldn't remember where it was. Then he found it in his pocket after all. He dawdled downstairs, filling it – and Mrs Hurry-Up appeared from the kitchen.

"Hurry-Up told me to tell you he had started for the bus," she said. "Run, or you won't catch it!"

Dawdle was not used to running. He puffed and panted and panted and puffed and do you know, when he reached the corner, the bus had just gone! There it was, rattling off down the lane.

"Oh my!" said Dawdle. "When does the next bus go?"

"Not for four hours," said a passer-by. "You'll have to walk. You'll get to the market by lunch time."

Poor Dawdle set off. He simply didn't

dare to go back and face Mrs Hurry-Up. He thought he would walk all the way to the next town, ask for Mr Spickspan's house, and join Hurry-Up there for lunch. He was really beginning to feel very hungry indeed.

He walked fast for quite a long way. Then he began to dawdle. He looked at some men mending the road. He watched some cows in a field. He looked at a train running through a tunnel. He sat down and took a stone out of his shoe.

So, by the time he reached Mr Spickspan's house, he saw Hurry-Up running down the steps, waving goodbye to Mr Spickspan!

"Thanks for the nice lunch!" Hurry-Up was saying. "Oh, hello, Dawdle – you didn't come to lunch after all. I wondered where you'd got to. Come on, we've got to catch the train now. I've a meeting to go to."

But this was too much for Dawdle.

"I've got a train to catch too!" he said firmly, "but it's not your train, Hurry-Up!"

He ran off to the station – how he ran!
No dawdling about him then, for he was
so afraid that Hurry-Up would catch
him, and make him go to the meeting.
Always hurrying, hurrying, hurrying to
something!

Dawdle actually caught his train with
five minutes to spare. He hid under the
carriage seat till the train went out, for
he was so afraid that Hurry-Up might
come to look for him. Then, when the

train puffed out of the station, he crawled out, much to the astonishment of two old ladies, and sat down in peace.

Mrs Dawdle was so surprised to see him. "You are soon home again!" she said. "How did you get on?"

"We won't talk about it, wife," said Dawdle. "In future I will try and be quicker – but not so quick as Hurry-Up! It makes me out of breath even to think of him!"

Mrs Dawdle smiled to herself. She could quite well guess what had happened. She didn't say anything but whenever Dawdle is a bit lazier than usual, she says, "Oh, Dawdle – don't you think it would be nice to go and see your cousin Hurry-Up again?"

And then you should just see how Dawdle hurries his work! You'd hardly believe it!

I Don't
Want To!

Once upon a time there was a little girl called Fanny. She was eight years old, and she had been spoilt. She had been ill quite a lot, and because her mother had been sorry for her, she had let Fanny have her own way far too much.

Whenever she asked Fanny to do something she didn't like, the little girl would say "I don't want to!" and would pout and frown.

"Will you go and post this letter for me?" her mother would say. And Fanny would make the usual answer:

"I don't want to!"

Well, if you say a thing like that often enough, you just can't stop, and soon Fanny was saying "I don't want to!" a hundred times a day.

"What a spoilt child!" people said. "Really, she is most unpleasant!"

Her granny spoke sternly to her. "Fanny," she said, "I don't like this habit you have of saying 'I don't want to!' to everything. Do try and stop."

"I don't want to," said Fanny at once.

Well, well – what can you do with a child like that!

Now one day Fanny went across the fields and took a wrong turning. Soon she found herself outside an odd little house. A well stood nearby and an old woman was turning the handle which drew up the bucket of water. She saw Fanny and beckoned to her.

"Little girl, come and help me to get this water!"

"I don't want to!" said Fanny at once.

The old woman frowned. She wound up the bucket, took it off the hook, and set it down.

"You could at least carry it for me into the house," she said. "I'm feeling rather tired today."

"I don't want to!" said Fanny, of course.

148

"Well, what a horrid child!" said the old dame. "You can't seem to say anything else but 'I don't want to!' Can't you say something pleasant for a change?"

"I don't want to!" said Fanny.

"Very well – don't!" said the old woman. "Say 'I don't want to!' and nothing else! Maybe you will soon want to change!"

And with that she went up the path to her cottage, opened the door, went inside and shut the door after her. Fanny felt a bit frightened. She remembered that the old woman had green eyes. Perhaps she was one of the fairy folk!

She ran off, and soon found her path. She went back home and on the way she met Jane, a schoolfriend.

"Fanny! Come and play with me after tea and see my new doll!" called Jane.

"I don't want to!" said Fanny, much to her own surprise, because she did want to, very much indeed. Jane had told everyone at school about her new doll, which could stand up by itself, and say "Mamma!"

"All right, don't come then!" said Jane, offended. "I'll ask Mary."

Fanny walked home, upset. Her mother met her at the door.

"Fanny dear, go and get yourself a pennyworth of sweets before you come in," she said. "You didn't have your Saturday penny last week. Go and spend it now."

"I don't want to!" said Fanny, and made her mother stare in surprise. Fanny stared at her mother too. She hadn't meant to say that! She loved sweets and it was fun to go and buy them. She wanted to say "I do want to!" but all her tongue said was "I don't want to!" once again.

"My dear child, if you don't want to, you needn't!" said her mother. "How tiresome you are sometimes! I will give your penny to John next door."

Fanny walked up to her bedroom,

almost in tears. She passed her granny on the way.

"I'm making cakes," said Granny. "Come and scrape the bowl out, Fanny."

Now this was a thing that Fanny simply loved doing. But, as you can guess, all her tongue would answer was "I don't want to!"

"Well, I thought it would be a treat for you," said Granny, offended, and she marched off with her head in the air.

Poor Fanny! That was a dreadful day for her. It seemed as if everyone was offering something nice for her to do. And all she could say was "I don't want to!"

In the end everyone was cross with her and her mother sent her to bed. "Go up to bed and stay there!" she said.

"I don't want to!" said Fanny. But she had to go all the same.

Now when she was in bed, crying under the clothes, there came a tapping at her door – and who should come in the bedroom but the old woman who had been by the well.

"Good evening," she said to Fanny. "How have you been getting on with that tongue of yours? Wouldn't it be nice to speak properly again?"

Fanny couldn't answer, because she knew that if she did, her tongue would

say "I don't want to!" And she did badly want to speak properly again – very, very badly.

"Well now," said the old dame, "I'll make a bargain with you. If you try to be a nice little girl, and not spoilt and rude, I'll make your tongue right again. But I warn you that if you say 'I don't want to' more than once in a day, the spell will come back again and you'll find you can't say anything else but that!"

"Thank you," said Fanny. "I'm sorry I was rude to you. I won't be rude or spoilt any more."

"That's the way to talk!" said the old dame, and she smiled. "Goodbye! Come and see me another day, and maybe your tongue will say something nicer to me than 'I don't want too!'"

Well, Fanny found it very hard to get out of her bad habit, but as she knew quite well that the spell would come back if she said "I don't want to" more than once in a day, she was very, very careful. The spell hasn't come back, so maybe she will be all right now.

She is trying to find the old woman's cottage again to tell her that she has cured herself. I wish I could go with her. I'd like to see the old dame's green eyes twinkling at me, wouldn't you?

Mr Snoop's
Carrots

One dark, cold winter the village of Shiver was hungry – so hungry that some of the people began to look very thin.

"Our potatoes have gone bad," they said to one another. "The harvest was poor, too, so we have very little corn to make bread. It's no good asking the next villages to help us, for they are as badly off as we are."

"We had better all bring what we have got to the Mayor," said Dame Bent. "Some of us have turnips and carrots, some have corn, some have dried meat. Let us all bring what we have got, and then the Mayor can share it out between us so that we all have the same."

"Yes, that is a good idea," said Mother Bright-Eyes. "It will be fair to everyone."

156

Old Man Snoop didn't think it was a good idea at all. He had a whole cellarful of carrots, good orange carrots, and he didn't want to share them with anybody. There were enough there to make him soup for the whole winter – why should he share them with anyone else?

Everyone had to go to the Mayor and declare what he had in his cellars or larder. Then, the next day, the Mayor would send men to collect the things, and after that they would be stored and doled out through the cold, hungry winter.

Mr Snoop went to declare what stores he had. "A dozen carrots," he said in a doleful voice, "and a packet of tea, a little sugar, and a little dried meat."

"Why, Mr Snoop, you have hundreds and hundreds of carrots," said Dame Bent, at once. "You know you have! Surely you are not thinking of keeping those for yourself? A dozen carrots, indeed! I hope the Mayor's servants will explore your cellars well and take away all your carrots! You're a nasty, mean old man."

"I am not!" said Mr Snoop, feeling angry because everyone had heard what Dame Bent had said. "I have only about a dozen carrots, as I said, and the Mayor's servants can certainly explore my cellars! And, to prove that I am not mean, I say this – I will only take from the Mayor exactly half the food he gives to others. So there!"

There was a silence after these words. People didn't know what to think. Could Mr Snoop have a cellar full of carrots if he was willing to let others look and see?

And could he be so mean as they thought if he offered to take only half the food that everyone else was having?

"Well, we'll see what we shall see," said Dame Bent, and she turned away. She told the Mayor to be sure to tell his servants to look at Old Man Snoop's cellars carefully next day for she did not trust him at all.

Old Man Snoop went home very angry. Now, because of that interfering Dame Bent he would have to hide all the carrots he had stored in his cellar!

"I'll put them into my barrow and wheel them to the middle of the Long Field, and dig a hole there and bury them," said Mr Snoop to himself. "I'll hide them all away and only leave about a dozen in the cellar. I shall be able to slip out each night and get some in for my soup – so I shall easily be able to manage on half the food that the Mayor gives to the others. Ha! They thought I was generous over that!"

That night Old Man Snoop wheeled many barrow-loads of carrots to the middle of the Long Field. He dug a big hole and buried them there. Then he marked the place with four white stones set together.

The next day the servants of the Mayor came round to everyone to collect what food they had. They came to Old Man Snoop's house and asked for the food he had in his larder and cellars. He flung open the doors.

"There you are!" he said. "Take what you see. I don't wish to keep anything back."

There were only a dozen carrots in the cellar! "He told the truth," whispered one servant to another. "Dame Bent was wrong."

The next day everyone went to the storehouse to get their ration of food, Old Man Snoop too. He asked for only half, for he had made up his mind to appear very good and generous. "And don't give me any carrots, please, because I don't like them at all," said Mr Snoop, in a loud voice, hoping that Dame Bent would hear him. "They give me a dreadful pain. On no account give me carrots."

He knew he would have plenty of carrots of his own to eat! Clever Mr Snoop!

That night Snoop went to fetch himself a few carrots for soup, and he had a very good meal, far bigger than anyone else in Shiver Village. He went to bed and slept soundly, for his meanness never worried him.

In the morning, what a surprise! The ground was deep in snow! It was still snowing when Mr Snoop looked out of the window, and it snowed all day.

Well, that was the end of Mr Snoop going out to find his carrots! The four white stones that marked them were buried deep under the snow. He couldn't go digging down all over the field, for people would see the marks in the snow and guess what he had been doing. It was most annoying.

So Mr Snoop had to go without his carrots, and as he had only half the amount of food that everyone else had, he felt very hungry. What a mistake he had made!

"Never mind," he said to himself.

"When the snow goes I shall find my carrots again, and I shall be all right. I must go hungry for a few days."

During the snow the rabbits in the fields were very hungry too, for the grass was buried under the snow. But soon a rabbit smelled the pit of carrots, and it wasn't long before he had dug a tunnel to them, and told all his brothers and sisters about them.

The rabbits had a wonderful time eating the carrots; and then one morning Dame Bent, walking down the snowy path that ran round Long Field, noticed a bitten carrot lying on the snow. Then she saw another; and another. She followed them up and came to a big hole in the snow leading down to the pit of carrots, which was now uncovered by the rabbits.

"Look at that!" said Dame Bent, guessing that it was Old Man Snoop's hoard of carrots. "I must tell the Mayor, and he must send his men to collect such a lovely store of carrots. My, my, my!"

Well, the carrots were soon collected,

but Old Man Snoop didn't know that. He didn't get any of them, of course, because he had said that he didn't like carrots. He was very glad when the snow went, because now, he thought, he could go out and fetch in plenty of carrots from his store. And how hungry he was!

So, that night, when the weather had turned warm, and all the snow was melting, Old Man Snoop took his lamp and went out with a basket to find the four white stones that marked his pit of carrots.

But there were no carrots there except
for a few half-eaten ones that were hardly
any good at all. Old Man Snoop stood
there and wept.

"Oh, my carrots; oh, my lovely carrots!
The rabbits have got them. Oh, what a
dreadful thing."

The next day Mr Snoop went to the
storehouse with the others to collect his

food ration, and he saw piles and piles of carrots. Dame Bent saw him looking at them and smiled.

"Ah, Mr Snoop, what a pity you don't like carrots," she said. "These were found most unexpectedly in the middle of the field by your house. Extraordinary, wasn't it? Everyone is getting a good share of them each day except you; and, of course, you don't like carrots."

So poor Mr Snoop had to go without his carrots, after all; and, as he only had half the food that other people had, he felt very hungry and miserable indeed all that winter.

How glad he was when the cold weather went and springtime came, with its new stocks of green food and salad and rhubarb. How he gobbled everything up!

"I'll never be so mean again," he thought, as he sat down to a rhubarb pie. "I'm so thin that my bones rattle against one another, and all because I was mean and greedy, and wouldn't share with others. I don't think I deserved to lose all my carrots like that, all the same."

But he did, of course; and it was a very good thing, too, that he lost them, because it cured him of some very nasty ways, didn't it?

Poor
Lucy Loll!

Have you heard the strange tale of poor Lucy Loll? I'll tell you; it is really very funny.

Lucy Loll never stood up straight if she could lean against anything. She never sat straight on a chair but lolled forward. She couldn't stand by anything without lolling against it – so you see she had a very good name.

Her mother and her teacher used to get so cross with her. "Lucy, if you loll about like that you will never have a nice straight back," said her mother.

"Lucy, sit up straight and don't loll!" her teacher said each morning at school. "Haven't you any bones in you at all? The way you loll about makes me think your bones are made of butter!"

169

But Lucy Loll didn't take much notice. She was a lazy girl, and couldn't be bothered to sit up straight or stand nicely.

Now, one day Lucy's mother went to speak to Mrs Lucky, an old, old woman who lived on the top of Breathing Hill. She sometimes did mending, and she was known to be very wise. Lucy's mother took her some curtains to mend, and sat down in the neat little kitchen to have a chat.

Lucy Loll's mother said to Mrs Lucky that she did wish she knew how to cure Lucy of lolling about. It was so dreadful to see a little girl leaning on everything, and lolling over chairs and tables.

Mrs Lucky listened with a twinkle in her eye.

"You should send Lucy on a visit to see my sister, Dame Twiddle, in Loll-Town," she said. "She'd soon be cured there. There's a bus that goes every Saturday at ten to twelve from outside my cottage."

So Lucy's mother thought she would do this. She told Lucy to take some butter and eggs to Dame Twiddle, Mrs Lucky's sister in Loll-Town.

"You can catch the bus that leaves just outside Mrs Lucky's at ten to twelve tomorrow," she said. "It will be a little trip for you."

Lucy was pleased. She loved going on buses. At ten to twelve the next day, which was Saturday, she was waiting outside Mrs Lucky's cottage for the bus. Lucy was rather surprised to hear that a bus passed by there, for Mrs Lucky's cottage was only in a little lane that ran to the top of the hill and down the other side. It was not on the main road at all.

The bus came right to the minute. It

was a strange looking bus, for it was bright blue, with little yellow wheels, and the driver wore a red top hat. The conductor wore a yellow top hat and seemed to spend all his time running up and down the little stairway that led to the top of the bus. Lucy was astonished to see that there was a green stair carpet laid on the steps. She thought it a very grand sort of bus.

She got in. The conductor took her money, and gave her a rainbow-coloured ticket with *Loll-Town* printed on it. Lucy sat and looked out of the window. She didn't recognise the country they were passing through. It seemed different from what she was used to. The houses were smaller, very crooked and quaint. The road wound in and out like a river.

"Loll-Town! Loll-Town!" shouted the conductor, and Lucy got off the bus. The conductor waved his yellow top hat to her and the bus went on. Lucy looked round and wondered where Dame Twiddle lived.

Just where Lucy was standing was a

tall lamppost, painted yellow. Lucy waited by it till someone came past. She lolled up against it in the way she usually did – and the lamppost fell over with a crash!

Lucy stared in horror! A policeman came up and spoke sternly to her.

"Did you push that over?"

"No," said Lucy, "I just leaned against it and it fell."

"Then don't do it again," said the policeman crossly, and began to put the lamppost up again. Lucy ran down the street, frightened.

She came to where a man with a barrow was selling apples. Lucy thought he might know where Dame Twiddle lived. She stood by the barrow while the man weighed out some apples for a customer. And then, of course, Lucy lolled up against the barrow!

Over it went! The apples rolled across the road and the man shouted in anger and surprise. "What did you do that for, you naughty little girl? Turning my barrow over like that! I'll spank you if I catch you!"

Lucy ran off at once. She couldn't think how it was that the barrow had fallen over! Why, she had only just leaned against it for a moment!

She turned a corner. No one was in sight. Lucy wondered what to do. There was a red letterbox nearby and she went over to it. Perhaps someone would come and post a letter, or the postman would empty the letterbox and she could ask him where Dame Twiddle lived.

She lolled up against the red letter-box. Goodness gracious! It rolled over into the street and fell with a fearful crash! Lucy stared in horror.

The street ran down a hill – and do you know, that round red letterbox began to roll down the hill! *Swish-swish* went all the letters inside as it rolled, getting faster and faster! Lucy couldn't possibly stop it.

It went on and on down the hill and rolled into the village pond at the bottom with a terrific splash. Every one came running out of their houses to see it.

"Who rolled our letterbox down the hill into the pond?" they shouted. "Who did it?"

Lucy ran off quickly. She knew she hadn't meant to do such a dreadful thing. However could it have happened? She only just leaned against the letterbox for half a moment!

She came to another street. There were lots of people there. Lucy waited for a little boy to come up to her, and then she spoke to him.

"Can you tell me where Dame Twiddle lives?" she asked. And do you know, as she spoke she lolled up against the wall of the nearby house.

You can guess what happened! The house fell down at once! It tumbled down like a pack of cards, making a dreadful noise and sending clouds of dust up into the air.

Lucy got such a shock that she took

to her heels and ran away at top speed,
bumping into people and crying with
fright. She had knocked down a house!
What would people say?

An old lady spoke kindly to her:
"What's the matter, little girl?"

"Oh," said Lucy, drying her eyes, "I want to find Dame Twiddle's house and I can't."

"Well, I am Dame Twiddle," said the old lady, "and this is my house. Come inside."

Lucy was pleased. She went inside the dear little house. The kitchen was very spick-and-span. There was a table in the middle, two armchairs nearby, a big cupboard of china, a washtub with clothes soaking in it, and a dresser.

"I've brought you some butter and eggs from my mother," said Lucy, putting the basket down. "Mummy knows Mrs Lucky, your sister."

"Oh, do sit down," said Dame Twiddle, opening the cupboard door. "I'll get you a cake and some lemonade. It's so kind of you to come and see me."

Lucy didn't sit down. Instead she lolled against the kitchen table and, of course, it at once doubled up its legs and fell over. Poor Mrs Twiddle jumped so much that she dropped the glass she was holding and it broke.

178

"I'm sorry," said Lucy, and she tried to set the table up again. It seemed to help her, and in another minute was standing up quite all right. And then, of course, Lucy began to lean against the washub!

Over it went – *splish-splash*! The soapy water shot all over the floor and soaked Lucy's shoes and socks. Dame Twiddle was angry.

"Careless girl!" she said. "Wipe up the mess, please. First you knock the table over, then you knock the washtub down!"

Lucy went red. She took a cloth and mopped up the mess. And, would you believe it, no sooner had she finished than she went and leaned against the dresser.

And that fell over too. My goodness me, the crashing and smashing of cups and saucers and plates was simply dreadful!

Lucy took one look at Dame Twiddle's angry face and decided to run out of the door. She felt certain that the old lady was going to spank her. So out she ran into the street and asked a little girl where the bus stopped that went back to her own home.

"Round the corner by the Town Hall," said the little girl. So off Lucy ran at top speed to catch the bus. It wasn't there, so the little girl waited by the big Town Hall.

Well – you know what she did, don't you? She leaned against the big building

– and down it went, like a heap of toy bricks! *Crash-smash-bang-clang.*

Every one ran up in a hurry, shouting and talking at the tops of their voices.

"The Town Hall's down! Who did it? It's fallen over!"

The policeman among the crowd suddenly caught sight of Lucy Loll. He ran over to her.

"Did *you* push it down?" he cried.

"I – I – I didn't mean to!" wept Lucy.

"I only just leaned against it, please."

"Well, don't you know this is Loll-Town, and leaning and lolling are forbidden?" cried the angry policeman. "Just see the damage you do! Can't you stand up straight? Why must you lean and loll everywhere? You'd better get away from Loll-Town quickly!"

At that moment up came the blue bus with little yellow wheels. Lucy ran to it and jumped on. It raced down the street, and the little girl sat down thankfully.

"Fares please," said the conductor, raising his yellow top hat to her. Lucy paid him. She got off at Mrs Lucky's cottage and Mrs Lucky waved to her from the gate.

"Did you like Loll-Town?" she cried with a twinkle in her eye.

"It was horrid!" shouted back Lucy. "Everything fell down as soon as I leaned against it."

Mrs Lucky laughed and laughed. Lucy sped home as fast as she could.

She told her mother about her strange adventure. "Mummy, I shall never dare to loll against anything again," she said. "Suppose I leaned against our house and it fell down! Whatever would we do?"

"I really don't know," said Mother. And do you know, from that day to this Lucy Loll has sat up straight, and hasn't lolled once. She says if you know anyone who lolls, send her a card, and she will tell you where that strange blue bus can be caught to Loll-Town.

That
Garden Gate!

"Sheila, if you leave the garden gate open again I shall be very cross," said her mother. "You left it open yesterday and the hens got in and scratched and scraped over my seed bed. And you left it open when you went to school this morning and a horse came in and ate half Daddy's cabbages."

"Oh, bother! I do try to remember," said Sheila, crossly. "But I've got so many things to think of. Gates are a nuisance."

"Well, I have plenty of things to think of too," said Mother. "Please remember to shut the gate, Sheila!"

Sheila pouted. All the time it was "Remember this, don't forget that!" Had Mummy forgotten she was in the play at school, and had the chief part? It was very, very difficult to learn such a long part. How could she possibly remember such silly things as gates?

Sheila changed the subject. "Mummy, what about my clothes for the play? Have you made them yet?"

"I should have got on with them better this morning if I hadn't spent half an hour chasing the horse out of the garden," said Mother, still cross.

"Mummy, you know I'm the fairy queen in the play, don't you?" said Sheila.

"It's a lovely part, Mummy. You'll be awfully proud of me when you see me. Oh, I do hope you can make me a really lovely frilly dress – with silver wings and long white stockings, and a sash that ties all round me."

Mummy was never cross for long. She smiled at Sheila. "Well, I've unpicked a frilly white silk dress of your aunt's – yards and yards in it – and I'll make you a beautiful dress of that. And I'll make a blue silk sash out of an old silk petticoat of mine – and silver wings out of cardboard covered with silver gauze from an old evening coat. I'll borrow your cousin's long white stockings. How will that do?"

"It sounds lovely," said Sheila. "Oh, Mummy, shan't I look fine!"

Her mother worked hard at Sheila's clothes for the play. She made a lovely frilly dress out of the white silk, and she sewed a broad blue sash for it. She spent a long time making the silver gauze wings, and last of all she borrowed the white stockings from Sheila's cousin.

186

She tried the dress on Sheila. It looked lovely. She tied the sash round and then put on the wings. "Well, you really look very nice," she said. "Today I'll wash them and hang them on the line to dry. Then tonight I'll iron them, and they will be all ready for tomorrow."

Mother was as good as her word. She washed out the frilly dress and the silver gauze wings. She had already cut out the cardboard lining for them, to make them stand out stiff. She would sew that into the wings tomorrow. She washed the stockings and the blue silk sash.

She hung everything on the line to dry. "I'll take them in this evening and iron them all," she thought. "Then they will be ready for tomorrow. How sweet Sheila will look! I shall be so proud of her."

They hung drying in the wind all that day. After tea Sheila's mother put on her hat and called to Sheila. "Sheila, come and walk with me to Granny's. I'm taking her some eggs and things and you can help to carry them."

"Coming, Mummy!" called Sheila. "You start. I'll catch you up."

So Mother set off by herself. In a few minutes Sheila caught her up and she took the basket. Granny was very pleased to see them and heard all about the play next day, and Sheila's lovely fairy queen clothes.

"We really must go if I'm to get that ironing done," said Mother at last. "Come along."

Off they went, over the fields, down the lane and up to the gate. Usually there were some goats with their little kids playing on the common nearby, and Sheila looked for them as she always did. She liked the pretty little kids. But they weren't there. Perhaps someone had taken them to another place.

The garden gate was swinging open. Sheila frowned. Bother! She had forgotten to shut it again when she had run after her mother. She went in and her mother followed. "We'll take the things off the line before we go in, Sheila," she said.

But someone else had been before them. Someone else had taken them off the line – dragged them off the line – nibbled them – eaten them!

Sheila gave a loud scream. "Mummy! The goats! They've got into the garden – and found my fairy clothes. They've got them off the line. Look, look, they're half-eaten. And they've eaten all the silver wings, except this tiny little bit. Oh, Mummy, Mummy!"

She caught up a stick and flew at the three big goats and the four little kids in a rage.

Her mother went up to her and took away the stick. "Wait, Sheila," she said. "Wait before you punish anyone. Whose fault was this? How did the goats get in? Who left the gate open?"

Well, what could Sheila say to that? She rushed indoors, sobbing. The goats and the kids fled out of the garden in alarm, a bit of blue sash hanging out of the biggest goat's mouth. What a wonderful time they had had!

Mother gathered up the bits and pieces

sadly. All her work gone for nothing! What a shame!

She went to comfort Sheila. "I'm sad too," she said. "I worked hard on those clothes for you, Sheila. All my work is wasted."

Sheila flung her arms round her mother. "Mummy! It's a shame! You made them so beautifully. Now they're gone and I can't wear them. And it's all my fault!"

Well, so it was. Now she'll have to wear her ordinary dress in the play and she will be very sad. I'm sorry for her, aren't you?

The goats were sorry too. They all felt very ill in the night, poor things!